I0534817

BONDS AND BLOOD

THE MISTS OF ELISTA TRILOGY, BOOK 1

CLARA WILS

Gryphon's Gate Publishing

Bonds and Blood

Copyright © 2022 Clara Wils

Gryphon's Gate Publishing

550 King St. N.

PO Box 42088 Conestoga

Waterloo, ON

N2L 6K5

ISBN: 978-1-988115-97-9

Print ISBN: 978-1-988115-98-6

CHAPTER 1

WHERE DOES MY STORY START? OH, IT WAS QUITE SOME TIME ago. So much has happened, let me see what I can remember.

I suppose it starts in the year I had three names. Before that is... mostly prologue. But that year, everything changed. That year, my first name... was Sara. A normal name, a common name, and definitely not the name of a True-Bonded. Yet on that breezy spring day in the twenty-ninth year of the reign of Queen Whitewing, it was my dearest and deepest hope that I'd soon lose that name.

I PRAYED TO THE HIGH SPIRITS THAT TODAY I'D BE CHOSEN.

At twenty years old, it was my last chance. I'd be too old next year. There were only a few others my age in the milling group of perhaps two hundred youths in the Miraline village square. The rest were younger, fifteen or sixteen, and being particularly tall, I stood a full head above most here. Few returned if they weren't Chosen in their first couple years. Yet I was determined. I had to be Chosen, because for me... there was nothing else.

I had no desire — nor skill — to be a tradesperson or a farmer. I definitely didn't want to be "some man's wife". When I married it would be for love, not to have a man support me because I lacked in skill or education.

To be fair, I didn't lack education. If anything, I far exceeded most in that department. I was the foster daughter of a pair of scholars who worked at the Library of Miraline, and had received the benefit of their vast learning. I wasn't bright, like my foster sister — the actual daughter of my foster parents — and hadn't picked things up quickly. But they'd been persistent in their attempts to teach me and eventually most of it had sunk in.

I wasn't pretty, or witty, or charming like some girls. I was educated but had no real-life skills. If I wasn't Chosen...

No.

I have to be Chosen.

The mayor of Miraline — a True-Bonded artist named Kestrel — mounted the platform at the far end of the square and a hush fell over the murmuring crowd of youths. Even the encircling ring of parents went quiet. My parents weren't there. My birth parents had died when I was young. My foster parents were... as usual... at the library, working. It's not that they didn't care, they did, but their studies were important and usually came first. I'd long ago accepted that.

The mayor was resplendent in a green dress, which set off her fiery red hair. Smiling, she raised her hands and the crowd knew she was about to speak.

"Families from Miraline and the villages of the North. You all know what today means, so I will not belabor the details. Instead, I welcome our wonderful companions from The Mistlands, the Lumani, to begin The Choosing!"

And there they were.

The Lumani floated over the crowd of youths, appearing

as glowing orbs, anywhere from the size of a small coin to that of a grapefruit. They were creatures of light and Anima, the mystical energy of The Mistlands. And I hoped and prayed that one of these Lumani would Choose me. My ticket out of this town and into a Noble House. It wasn't the most selfless and noble of goals, but supposedly that didn't matter. What mattered was a person's spirit. I hoped one of them would sense something in my spirit today.

However, of the almost two dozen or so Lumani floating over us, none headed in my direction. The Choosing could take some time. The Lumani might stop and consider several people, using their mind-voice to interview them, before finally settling on their Chosen.

Signaling, waving, jumping up and down, none of these things were permitted. We had to stand there as still as possible for the Lumani, as they hovered over us.

The time ticked by. The large clock, to one side of the city square, slowly marked the seconds... then minutes. Two hours were allotted for The Choosing, and I was sweating with anxiety after the first hour passed. By my count, thirteen children had been Chosen by then. That left — at a quick count — ten Lumani.

To take my mind off the minutes ticking down on my fate, I tried to observe and categorize the Lumani still floating around.

Three were rather large. We were told the size of a Lumani meant nothing, but most people still assumed the larger the Lumani the more powerful it was. Of these three, two were darker shades, a deep rose-maroon and a stunning purple. I'd love to be Chosen by that one, such a royal color! The last of the three was a pale yellow, near to white.

Five Lumani were of various middling sizes, like apples and plums. Of those, two stood out: bright red and sky-blue.

The last two were quite small, the size of cherries. One of those was a mottled red and blue, and the last a soft cream-yellow, and... it was heading my way!

I vibrated with excitement, but tried to be as still as possible as they floated closer, heading straight for me.

Then they stopped, hovering over the young girl in front of me. She blinked up at the tiny glowing orb. "Oh, hello!"

I caught one side of the strange conversation that then took place.

"I want to go on adventures! Perhaps be a sea captain or wilderness explorer!" the girl said. Then she paused as she listened to the Lumani speak into her mind.

"Because there's so much of this world to see. Wouldn't you want to see the world?"

Another pause.

"Ah... well... I'm quick to learn new things."

Ha! Everyone said that.

"And... I... uh... I have a heart for adventure and excitement. Yeah, I'm brave, that's it!" She seemed to be struggling now, reaching for the *right* answer.

Then suddenly the girl's shoulders fell. "Oh," she said a bit forlorn. "I... understand."

She'd been turned down. Perhaps another Lumani would Choose her, but not this little yellow one.

That Lumani began to float away. I panicked, my hope crumbling. I pictured myself reaching out to them, all my desires expressed in one imagined gesture.

The Lumani stopped, then circled back to me.

Oh Spirits! This is it! This was the first time one had even stopped to speak with me. I had to make a good impression I had to... but suddenly my mind drained of any useful and intelligent information and I was left a gibbering idiot.

"Hello?" I said pre-emptively.

Hello, child. The voice was calm, sedate, but resonating power.

Oh Spirits, oh Spirits, oh Spirits! They were actually talking to me!

Tell me, child, what do you want?

"I... ah..." Bloody bones! What did I want? "I..." Oh no, I was screwing this up, I'd never get this one to Bond with me!

Be calm, child. I got the sense of laughter, a faint chuckle. *Take a deep breath, and you'll remember. What do you want?*

I did as instructed, taking a long breath, and words came to me. "I want to be important." *Bloody bones! No! That wasn't the right answer.* I had to say something else. "I need to... I need..." Was this why none of the others had Chosen me in the past five years? Because I didn't have clear life goals? How was I supposed to know what I wanted? True, I was a full-grown woman, but still...

Perhaps I should ask a different question. If we were joined, what would you seek as your True Calling?

That I could answer. "I want to be a Noble. I want to join one of the Noble Houses and be a part of ruling Elista!" I'd finally managed a coherent sentence.

The small Lumani floated there for a long moment, saying nothing, and I began to wonder If I'd offended them somehow. I tried not to say anything. I feared I might offend them further.

Finally, they spoke again.

Why do you wish to be a Noble?

I hesitated. Closing my eyes, I drew a deep breath to steady myself, searching for the right words. "I do not seek power. I do not know yet, how best I might serve our nation, but that is what I truly wish to do, be of service and help to keep Elista as the peaceful and prosperous nation it is."

Again, there was a long pause.

I will not ask your name, child, for the name you held shall soon be a memory. I Choose you, child. The Lumani gave a weird chuckle-sigh. *I think you and I will do well together. You are driven and dedicated, even if you do not know what you are driven towards. But your spirit calls to me, child, and I hope we can be one. My name is Auwei.*

I was too stunned to say anything.

I'd been Chosen!

This way, child, Auwei said serenely and began bobbing away. I followed, as if in a trance. This was it. I'd finally been Chosen.

Now... I just had to prove I was worthy.

CHAPTER 2

Do you have anyone you need to tell? Auwei's voice in my head snapped me out of my shocked reverie.

"Uh... yes, my parents... well foster parents."

Take what time you need. A carriage will be waiting for us when you're ready.

Yes, the carriages. A line of carriages had taken up one end of the town square, waiting to take the Chosen to Silverveil, the academy where Chosen worked to become True-Bonded. Only a few remained. One of them was for me.

Spirits and Sprites, this is happening!

I was still so agitated it took me a long moment to remember what had caused me to look for the carriages: leaving... and telling someone I was leaving! *Oh, right!*

This way, child. Auwei floated ahead of me to a long table with several sheets of parchment and sticks of charcoal. Sitting behind the table was Elder Madrin. The old man smiled at me.

"I'm glad you were Chosen, Sara." He laughed. "Though I suppose I won't be calling you that the next time I see you."

He sighed. "Your parents will be so happy. Is there a message you want to write for them?"

"Yes, thank you," I said, taking one of the sheets and a stick of charcoal. The Elder was there for any children who didn't know how to write yet. He could scribe a note for them if their family wasn't here. Since young people came from all around Miraline for The Choosing, and most were uneducated farmers, that was a common occurrence.

I hesitated, my fingers fidgeting on the coal, getting dark and grimy. What would I say? The Clarks had taken me in at the age of six. I only had faint memories of my real parents. The Clarks had been there for my formative years... and yet not been there. Their primary concern for their children had been a solid education in various disciplines. Other than that, they'd been buried in their own work illuminating and scribing manuscripts.

My sister Ella — though now her name was Dove — and I had been left to ourselves for much of our youth. We'd grown up a bit free and wild. It hadn't been a bad life, but it hadn't been a truly warm one either. I was closer with Dove than I was with our parents. Still, they had done so much for me.

I put the charcoal to the parchment and quickly wrote, "Thank you for everything. I was Chosen. I'll write when I can. I love you."

Short, simple, and sweet, Auwei said.

I handed the parchment to Elder Madrin, who smiled. "I'll make sure it gets to them right away." He worked with them at the library, so he'd see them soon enough.

With that, I turned and headed for the line of carriages.

I had everything I needed with me in a satchel: my favorite book — hand-written by my foster parents of course — as well as a few dresses and some odds and ends.

"Sara?"

I turned at my name and was surprised to see my foster father, Edrid Clark, hurrying up to me. I was so stunned I couldn't move until he swept me up in a hug.

"I'm so happy for you!" he said on the verge of tears.

"Where's mother?" I asked, but I knew she wouldn't be here.

"She couldn't bear to see you leave, or see you unchosen." As I'd suspected. "But I... I had to know and see you one last time if you were. Spirits Within! I'm so happy for you. I know you wanted this so much." He hugged me tighter, lifting me from the ground for a moment. When he set me down, he looked at Auwei.

"Thank you," he said to the Lumani. "She will do right by you. I've never seen a girl with more spirit!" He blushed a little, perhaps realizing what he'd just said. He looked at me. "Don't tell Dove I said that, but it's true. I love my daughters both, but you always had a bit more fire in you than she did. She was so bright of mind, and you of spirit."

I think that was the kindest thing he'd ever said to me. I slipped in to give him a long hug, tears in my eyes. "Thank you for everything. I love you, Papa."

"I know, Sara. And I'm happy you got what you wanted. Go and shine in your new life as much as you have brightened ours."

I squeezed him tighter, not able to say anything. It was a long moment before I could choke out the words, "Good-bye, Papa."

I released him and was just a bit surprised to see his cheeks as wet with tears as mine. He was usually such a stoic man.

He nodded. "Good-bye." Then he stepped back, holding me at arms-length as if to get one last look at me. I took the moment to do the same. He had ink smudges on his smooth cheeks, a smile on his wide mouth, and a softness to his brown eyes as his unkempt blond hair tousled about his brow.

"I'll return when I can," I said, though in truth I had no clue when that might be. Ella — now Dove — my sister, had been Chosen three years ago and had yet to return.

He nodded with a sad smile.

We stood there for a moment longer before he released me. I took that cue and turned, marching to a carriage. When I stepped up, half through the open door, I looked back.

He waved.

I waved.

Then I stepped into the coach and the driver closed the door.

This was it.

That was very sweet. I knew you were the right choice, Auwei said and glowed just a bit brighter. I hadn't thought that possible, but her cream-yellow color became just a bit more distinct and vivid. Then she giggled.

Giggled?

Were Lumani supposed to giggle?

Also... when had I started thinking of her as a "she"? The voice in my head did sound distinctly feminine, but the Lumani had no genders.

It is well, child, you can think of me as a "she" if you like. I have Chosen nearly all female Bonded in my many lives. And the two men I Chose were both, well... not like other men, let's say. So, I guess I've usually been a female once I'm Bonded. Another giggle. *And I guess I will be again soon enough.*

I was a little taken aback by this.

The carriage began to move.

"Auwei...?" I wasn't sure what to say. I thought the Lumani were a bit more composed and serene and majestic.

More giggling. *Once you've lived as many lifetimes Bonded to humans as I have, you pick up a few quirks. Sorry child, but you're gonna have to live with them if we're to be Bonded. I hope I didn't give you the wrong impression earlier. I like to be serious when Choosing.* I got the sense of a shrug. *But this is the real me.*

"The real you?"

Yup, the real me. And I think we'll work well together.

"You do?" I suppose I was a bit irreverent and wild.

Yup.

"Is that why you Chose me? Because I'm..." I didn't know how to say it.

Yes and no. That was one factor, the other, as your father pointed out, was your spirit. For a long time during The Choosing, you didn't stand out, but then there was a flash as I passed you, something bright and powerful. And as I spoke to you, I tried to draw that out. You keep it well hidden, but I know it's there. That's why I Chose you.

"Oh." That was a bit of a surprise. Before today I'd not thought of myself as anyone with a special spirit, but now... perhaps...

And that's what we'll work on when we get to Silverveil, your spirit. In order to make a True-Bond, we need to connect on that level. Also, we'll need to find what avatar you've Chosen for us.

I was excited to find my avatar, the animal form Auwei — and later myself — would take. The shape that would give me my true name. I hoped it was something as lovely as my sister, Dove, or as powerful as Skyfire — a wyvern — the leader of Wyvern House.

Auwei giggled again. *We'll just have to wait and see, won't we!*

Now, there are a few things you'll need to know before we get to Silverveil, Auwei said, becoming a bit more serious in tone. *Or perhaps you already know? What do you know of the process of True-Bonding?*

Time to bring out my extended education. I had learned a fair bit from my parents, but it had been my sister, who had gone through this process three years ago — and written to tell us all about it — from whom I'd learned the most about Bonding.

"All the newly Chosen will come together and live for a time at Silverveil. There is a girls' dorm and boys' dorm, and any fraternizing between them is frowned upon. We're supposed to be spending our time with our Lumani, not snogging behind the dining hall."

Auwei snorted and laughed a heavy guffaw at that. *That's an interesting way of putting it, but yes. Go on.*

Snorting? She'd actually snorted? This was going to be truly interesting.

"Once there, we'll work to bring out our avatar, our True Shape," I continued. "When we do, you'll assume that shape at first. Once you have, we will begin to work on Bonding. Unfortunately, no one, human or Lumani, truly understands how it works, it just does. We'll either Bond or we won't." But I didn't want to think of that option.

Still, Auwei brought it up.

Yes, that is perhaps the most important part of the time we'll spend at Silverveil. We must Bond during those three months. If we don't, it will never happen. She gave a heavy sounding sigh. *That has only happened to me once. It was... painful for both of us.* She perked up a little then. *I'm sure that won't happen with you!*

If it did, I'd have to return to Miraline, and I would never be Chosen again, even if I hadn't been too old. Some people were just not Bondable. If you failed out of the Bonding, even if you were young enough to try again the next year, you were banned from returning. Some people recovered from that and went on to lead productive lives. Others... didn't. I was certain I wouldn't recover. I knew if this didn't work out, I'd... well... it just had to work out.

I drew in a long breath, banishing those thoughts. "Right! I'm sure we'll be a good match!"

Exactly! What else do you know of Silverveil?

"Silverveil is more of a school than a village, though there is a village nearby, mostly to serve the needs of the school. Also, it's called Silverveil because it's so close to The Mistlands, your home."

The Mistlands may be where I come from, but I do not know if I consider them my home anymore. I have spent nine lifetimes in your world and much prefer it to The Mistlands now. Everything here is more... solid. I have come to like the tactile senses of you humans, they're so much more visceral and immediate.

"Oh...?" This was a bit of a surprise. The Mistlands were a mystical place and I couldn't imagine not wanting to be a part of them. "Do you think I could see The Mistlands?"

Yes, of course, we'll go at some point while we're at Silverveil. All Chosen need to see it to help them understand us.

That would be amazing! Being in the realm of The Spirits.

There wasn't that much more I knew about Silverveil. Dove had told us a lot, but not much on the details of how the Bonding actually worked, or the day-to-day activities. But there was one last thing she had mentioned.

On the bench of the carriage opposite me was an envelope. I picked it up and opened it to find three heavy cards within. "And I know what these are, my sister told me about them," I said.

The first card indicated my name during my time at Silverveil. Each Chosen was given an interim name while there. We were no longer who we'd been, our lives had changed and our names should reflect that. And, with luck, we'd have our True-Bonded name soon enough.

My card read: "Birch."

"While I'm at Silverveil, until I get my True Name, I'll be called Birch."

Ooh! It must be fate! Auwei said excitedly. *I've worked with two others who were Birch's as well! Hello, Birch!*

I smiled at that. It did seem somewhat lucky or fated.

The second card said "Forest" on it.

"This is the name of the group of other Chosen I'll be working with. We work in small groups to help each other out. I'm in the Forest group."

"And this last will be the name of my instructor." I picked it up and read: "Lady Kitsune." I shrugged. That meant nothing to me. She would be a True-Bonded, but I didn't know what type of animal a Kitsune was.

A flying, many-tailed, foxlike animal, Auwei said matter-of-factly.

There were far more animals in the world than I could name, but that one was a surprise. "Oh."

Now you're all set, just sit back relax and enjoy the ride to Silverveil. Auwei sounded chipper and calm, but I sensed her tension. She was worried.

Was she worried about me? About the possibility of not Bonding? If so, that's what I was concerned about as well, and her worry didn't help me feel any better about my prospects.

CHAPTER 3

SILVERVEIL WAS A WONDEROUS PLACE. PERCHED ON A PLATEAU, high in the northern hills of Elista, next to the rushing waters of the Mist River, the walled compound captured the eye and the imagination. To the east was the famed Foggy Forest, where heavy mists clung to the lands at all times, the doorway to The Mistlands.

There was something mystical about this place. I could feel it as soon as the carriage passed through the gates. Perhaps it was all the Chosen and True-Bonded in one place. More than anywhere else in Elista, except during a conclave of the Noble Houses. I half-hung out the window of the carriage, eyes wide with wonder, gawking at the grounds and the many others milling around.

The Choosing in Miraline was one of several such events that happened all over Elista, which meant there were dozens of carriages arriving, disgorging passengers, and departing. It was chaos; beautiful, amazing chaos.

My carriage rolled to a stop and I was out the door before the coachman could open it.

I took a deep breath of the rarified air, catching the scent of the distant river and the pine forests. The same air so many before me had breathed. All True-Bonded came here to learn the ways of the Lumani and Bonding. Queen Whitewing and House Leader Skyfire may have stood in this very spot, or slept in the bed I'd be assigned.

My heart pounded so hard, I couldn't hear anything anyone was saying, even Auwei. I just spun in a slow circle taking everything in: the high walls, the many carriages, the Great Square in the middle of the grounds, the many low buildings. From Dove's letters, I thought I knew what each was. The closest, to the left of the gates, was an administration building. North of that would be the girls' dorm. Then a smaller building for the female instructors. The long building directly across campus from me would be the great hall and classrooms. And down the right side would be the male instructors building, the boys' dorm, and the stables and storage building, all perfectly symmetrically laid out.

Birch! Auwei's voice finally broke through my excitement. It took me another moment to realize she was speaking to me. I wasn't used to this new name yet. *There's someone just over there who's gathering the female Chosen.* Oddly, even though Auwei had no appendage with which to point, I knew exactly where she was indicating when she said "there."

I looked and saw a strict looking woman, to whom all the female Chosen seemed to be heading, and made my way toward her.

"What's your name?" I overheard a younger girl in a bright green dress say to another in a stunning blue dress.

"Cedar. Yours?"

"River!"

"At least yours sounds like a girl's name. I can't believe I got Cedar. And with my luck, I'll be stuck with a bunch of low-born dolts."

I hadn't really listened to anything past her name: Cedar, which meant she was probably in my Forest group. I veered off to speak to her.

Birch, no— Auwei tried to warn me.

"Hello," I said introducing myself to the girl in blue. She looked to be fifteen and was pristinely attired with perfect bouncing blond curls and eyes as blue as her dress. "My name is Birch. I'm guessing we're both in the forest group."

She stared at me like I had two heads. "You're old!" she scoffed. Then with derision: "Let me guess, you're from Miraline?" I didn't even answer before she nodded to herself. "I thought so." She turned her nose up at me like I smelled of midden, and made a point of making a wide arc around me to get to the harsh-looking woman admitting people.

Sorry, Auwei apologized with a sigh. *I recognized her type. Some here will be... entitled. Their family has probably been True-Bonded or Noble or both for generations. Some don't like new-bloods joining their ranks. If it's a Noble you wish to become, you'll probably face more like her.* Auwei sighed heavily. *It's something that hasn't changed over my nine lifetimes, unfortunately.*

I was still just a little shocked at that reception. I hadn't been the most popular girl in Miraline. Dove and I had been a bit freer and wilder than most of the other girls. When they'd been playing with dolls or learning needlework, we'd been playing with boys by the river, getting dirty and having adventures. Still, the girls of town usually just thought I was a bit odd, not... trash.

And suddenly all my wonder and awe came crashing down upon me as Auwei's words sank in.

Some don't like new-bloods...

... you'll probably face more like her.

It's something that hasn't changed over my nine lifetimes...

I'd thought myself invincible now that I was Chosen, but I was starting to see this was still only the very beginning of a long journey. I blinked a few times as this realization settled on me. But then...

Oooohhhh! Auwei said as if shivering. *I felt that.*

I'd felt it too, a hardening in my stomach, a core of resolve and rededication to my goals: True-Bonded, then Noble, then... maybe even someday... queen? I gave a hard, grim smile.

That, that right there. That's why I Chose you, Birch. And... oh! She sounded surprised, almost pained.

Auwei had been hovering just above my right shoulder, but she descended to settle on me as tiny tendrils sprouted from her spherical form. Those tendrils formed into legs; eight legs. A tiny cream-yellow glowing ball, with eight legs. Two over-large eyes appeared on the orb as well, blinking.

Auwei laughed. *You have Chosen our avatar, Birch. We're—*

No, please don't say what I think you're about to say.

—A spider.

Bloody bones! A spider? Really? I was certain that wasn't going to go over well with the other girls.

Spirits of the Mists! This was going to be a long three months.

I squared my shoulders, drew in a long breath, then headed for the admitting woman.

"Name," she barked, voice level and cold, as I drew up before her. She hadn't even looked at me.

"Birch."

She flipped through her lists and used a wrapped piece of

charcoal to check off a spot. "Primary dorm, room seventeen." She pointed, looking back toward the dorm. "You can go in that door there. Your room will be near the end of the hall on the left." Only then did her head swing back to look at me.

"Spirits Within! What is that?" She shrieked eyes going wide, pointing at Auwei.

She seemed to realize what she was seeing as I said the words: "That's my Lumani."

The woman blinked. "You've Chosen your avatar already?" She seemed an odd combination of astounded and disgusted, a shiver taking her.

I stood there a moment longer, wondering if there was more before she said, "Shoo, go! You know your room number, everything you need will be there." As I moved away, I caught her muttering, "Some young women these days! A spider? Truly?"

Ahead of me, Cedar and River had paused at the lady's outburst, then turned to each other and hurried ahead to the dorm. I had no desire to join them, so I made my way slowly, trying to savor and enjoy these first moments at Silverveil... and failing miserably.

I entered the dorm through a door at the end. Dove had mentioned that each Chosen got their own room. She'd been a bit stunned and surprised at that, seeing as she and I had shared a room for as long as I'd been with the Clark family. The doors down the left side of the hall had odd numbers starting with one, on the right side were even numbers starting with two. I looked ahead down the hall and caught Cedar and River giggling as they came out of a room, which — I couldn't quite tell from this distance — might be mine.

"Ooops!" Cedar called out to me. "Wrong room!" They

were hiding something from me. Had they taken something from my room?

There isn't much to take, Auwei said. *But those two certainly seem like they're up to no good.*

I shook my head as they exited the far end of the dorm. If Dove's letters were any indication, there would be a girl's common room at that end of the dorm with doors from this dorm and the secondary dorm, as well as a door leading outside. I didn't want to chase the girls, so I just went into my room to see what they might have done.

I didn't see anything out of place and sighed.

Hmmm, Auwei hummed softly. *I think I know what those girls did.*

"Oh?" I moved in. The room was narrow with a good-sized window on the far side, sunlight streaming in. Next to the window was a bed, its head against the far wall and its side against the right wall. To my right stood a large cabinet and desk unit. A narrow door, the full height of the cupboard was probably a small closet. Two more, smaller cabinets were situated over the desk area.

On the bed.

I moved in and looked at what Auwei had indicated, a single folded dress in a dark-blue-grey color.

Yup, just as I thought. Auwei sighed. *Those pesky girls stole the other sets of clothes that should be here. Every Chosen is provided with three sets to account for different sizes, a small, a medium, and a large set. There should also be a note here with instructions for what to do next. They've taken that too. I don't know what they thought to achieve, their Lumani must know that your Lumani would be aware of what should be here.* A heavy sigh. *Some Lumani...*

"What did the note say?"

To get dressed and meet in the Great Square. Assemble with your group at your instructor, who should have a sign of some sort.

"Ah, yes, I would have just sat here all evening, clueless."

But they must have known I'd know that, so their intent wasn't to stop you, just...

"Humiliate me." I lifted the single garment they'd left. It would be a tight fit on me, almost scandalous. If there had been three dresses, this must have been the small one. Being rather tall, I guessed I'd have wanted the large dress. As it was, an intriguing set of buttons down the front of the dress looked like it allowed for varying builds.

I laughed.

What?

"I'll show them. I'll wear it proudly."

Or, just a thought, you could ask one of the other girls in the dorm to borrow one of their dresses if they're not using their large one.

"No, this'll be more fun." I shrugged. "I'm guessing there aren't many here with my height and, with you as a spider, I'm already going to stand out. I might as well play that up." I stripped off my clothes and squeezed into the dress.

There's a looking glass on the inside of that long closet door.

I opened the cabinet door and found the looking glass on the back... and burst out laughing.

I'd never been all that busty, more athletic and slender. Still, this dress made me look like some wanton lady-of-the-night. It was skin tight over my bust, waist, and hips, buttons bulging. Even as I stood there, a button popped off, exposing my belly-button. Then there was the length, it covered my thighs at least, but only barely, ending at the knee.

Oh yes, I'd make quite an impression in this.

Are you sure you want to do this? I'm certain one of the other girls would allow you to borrow one of their dresses.

"No, we're doing this! In fact... how much time do I have before the meeting?"

An hour perhaps, maybe two. They'll ring a bell when it's time.

"Then I know exactly what I'm going to do." My mind was working. If these girls wanted to humiliate me, I'd show them. I'd own this, make it mine, make them see there was nothing they could do to hurt me...

And all the young men out there were in for quite a treat!

CHAPTER 4

THE BELL RANG FOR ASSEMBLY AND I STRUTTED OUT IN MY now custom-made dress. I'd altered it with a needle and thread I'd brought with me, raising the hemline.

You're going to be in so much trouble— Auwei said with a giggle. *I love it!*

Despite my show of confidence, I felt horribly self-conscious. I'd never done anything like this before. I was near to busting out of a dress with a hem so high I was having to work really hard to keep myself from not pulling it down.

Cedar and River wanted me to be embarrassed, ashamed, but I was going to turn this back on them and... probably make a name for myself in the process. I'd never wanted to be noticed before, but something in me had gone all hard and determined. I was already the tallest girl here; I might as well stand out in other ways.

Outside, the spring breeze was chilly on my naked legs, but I soldiered on.

Cedar was already with the Forest Group. She caught sight of me and her mouth fell open, eyes going wide. The two boys in our group — they looked to be no more than sixteen — had the same look on their face, mixed with a heavy dose of shame-lust.

I flashed them a grin.

Lady Kitsune, my instructor, was a woman of middle years with dark brown hair pulled back tight in a bun and severe grey eyes in a sharp-featured face. She was nearly as tall as I was and rail thin. When she caught sight of me, she nearly dropped the large sign saying "Forest".

"Spirits, girl! What's the meaning of this?" Her shock and horror were clear on her expression and in her tone. Two other girls in the group giggled.

I blinked innocently. "Oh, sorry, I..." I looked at Cedar. "My new friend Cedar here strongly suggested I wear this dress. I thought we were going to make it a group thing. I guess I was wrong."

Lady Kitsune flashed a look at Cedar. "This was your idea?"

The girl sputtered for a moment, clearly not expecting any of this. She finally stammered out, "N-no!"

Lady Kitsune swung her gaze back to me. "Get changed at once!"

I feigned ignorance. "Changed? But I only had this one dress." I turned to Cedar again. "You said we only got one dress each and had to make do."

Cedar sputtered again, eyes going wide.

Kitsune looked from me to Cedar and sighed. "Ah..." She didn't even ask Cedar if this was true, the confused guilt was clear from the heady blush on the girl's face. Kitsune sighed and looked at me again. "We'll get you a larger dress once we're done here. We have many." Shaking her head, she went on. "I believe we're all here?" There were just the six of us. "Please state your new names," Lady Kitsune asked.

"Birch, tall and pale, that's me," I cut in before anyone else could. One of the other girls laughed at that, the boys were still having a bit of trouble tearing their gazes off my legs.

"I'm Ash," one of the other girls said.

"Maple." This from the slightly taller of the two boys, who finally managed to look me in the eye, after a slow drawing up of his gaze over everything else. "Hi."

I flashed him a grin. "Hi."

Lady Kitsune made an odd strangled noise, then said, "Next!"

"I'm Oak," the other boy said and seemed to hesitate for a moment before adding: "That's a *hardwood* tree." He winked at me. The way he'd said that had made his innuendo clear.

I nearly choked — as did Lady Kitsune — trying not to laugh. I probably didn't hide my surprise well, but I reassessed Oak. He may have been the shorter of the two boys, but he was quick and probably older, perhaps eighteen?

"Good to know," I said with a nod, finally getting myself under control.

Oak smiled. He seemed to have gotten over his fascination with my legs, his gaze solidly on mine. Oh yeah, he could be trouble, and not just for me. Those clear blue eyes of his and that pristine beautiful young face would go over very well with most young women.

"None of that!" Lady Kitsune said harshly. Her composure cracked just a little. We were going to be The Bloody Pits for her. I could tell.

"Cedar," Cedar said finally, pulling herself up and trying —
and horribly failing now — to make herself stand out. She was
curvy yes, and beautiful with that well-styled blond hair and
those blue eyes, but I'd stolen all the attention away from her.

"Poplar," said the last girl, shy and giggly.

"Now!" Lady Kitsune snapped, trying to get focus back
on her. "Please also share the names of your Lumani."

"Auwei," I said indicating with my thumb the odd
cream-yellow glowing spider on my shoulder.

"You've already taken an avatar?" Oak said, nodding with
surprise and admiration. "Truly you're a woman well
advanced from the rest of us." Another wink from him.

"Hush boy!" Kitsune said.

"You mean she's old," Cedar said at the same time,
though both she and Lady Kitsune were spoken over by Oak
who continued:

"This is Oama." He indicated the large deep-blue ball
floating nearby.

The others went around without incident. Cedar's
Lumani was Eala, Maple's was Uesi, Poplar's was Aelo, and
Ash's was Iana.

"Now, for the rules and procedures here at Silverveil,"
Kitsune said, trying to regain control. She succeeded for the
most part, but Oak never took his eyes off me; neither did
Cedar, though for a completely different reason and with a
completely different look, full of contempt.

Lady Kitsune told us the times for the meals, and that
missing them would mean we'd go without. She said we'd
be working with her for the most part. Our mornings
would be spent in specific activities meant to help us
connect with our Lumani. There would be a few more
classes in the afternoons, then some free time before the
evening meals, during which we were expected to get to

know our Lumani further in ways better suited to our pairings.

She finished with a hard look at me and Cedar — apparently still not sure with whom she was more upset — and said, "Tomorrow seamstresses and tailors from the village will come to take your measurements. You'll have a set of custom clothes before the end of the week." She emphasized the next part. "You *will* wear those clothes and *not* modify them in any way! Is that clear?"

I smiled and nodded. "Clear."

We were then herded into the great hall for the evening meal, though I was escorted by Lady Kitsune herself to get me a new dress and change. The largest of the pre-defined sets was just a little loose on me, though with the way the buttons could be used to help them conform to a woman's figure I made it work well. This one came to just above my ankles. If nothing else, it would be warmer.

I ate only a little, having taken time away from the meal to change, but it was enough.

Then we were told to retire to our rooms for the evening in contemplation with our Lumani.

My contemplation didn't last long.

There came a soft knock on my window. I rose from where I'd been sitting on my bed and opened the heavy curtains.

Outside was Oak. He smiled and winked.

Curious, I opened the window, latching it up and leaning out on the sill to speak to him. "Yes?"

"Hey Legs, wanna go for a walk?" Oama bobbed excitedly next to him.

"Legs?"

"Yeah, most of the boys have taken to calling you that." He shrugged. "You can take it however you want, but from me, it's a compliment. You have nice legs... as well as every-thing else, that is."

Oh, he was a charmer.

And he was handsome enough, his clothes falling perfectly from broad shoulders, blue eyes sparkling, reflecting the lamp-light from my room.

"How did you know this was my room?" I asked.

He laughed. "I had to knock on a few other windows first, but eventually one of the others pointed me in the right direction." He gave me the full force of his charming smile.

"Might we go for a walk?" He asked with courtly manners. His voice grew hushed. "Or I could come in."

Something about him didn't sit right with me and I didn't want to give the impression I was interested. Sure, he was nice to look at, but... not really my type. Yet, after my stunt with the dress, I'd probably need to do a bit of image-mending.

"Not tonight, Oak," I said. I didn't want to cut him off entirely though, just let him know I had standards. A walk with a handsome young man wouldn't be so bad, though I probably wouldn't want anything more with him. So, I quickly added: "Once you and Oama have come up with an avatar, *maybe* I'll consider it." I hoped he heard the emphasis on "maybe."

He nodded. "Of course. I'd expect nothing less than to be a match for you before we might *go walking*." He drew himself up to his full height and gave a single nod. "I'll return in a few days. I'm sure we'll have found our avatar by then." He turned and left.

I shook my head. He was handsome enough and confi-dent, but... not my type. I liked my men just a bit less forward. Oak was too eager and almost arrogant in his approach. I'd always been a strong girl, now a strong woman, and I liked a man who let me know he was available, but let me do the pursuing.

Interesting. Auwei said, scurrying along the wall to the windowsill. *A rare man indeed, but I sense you've found such a man at least once, yes?*

"Yes," I confided as I closed the window. "There was a boy in Miraline, Kelen, who I grew up with. We were friends as children, then we became... more."

I sunk back onto the bed as memories returned like a flood. We had left the city on sunny afternoons and taken long walks in the fields around the town. At first, we'd talked. Then, as our bodies had matured, we'd explored each other, delving into our raging emotions. We'd bloomed together, learning and teaching, until our heated encounters were quite... rewarding. He'd been the first — and so far, the only — boy I'd been with.

But... then had come our first year of Choosing. We had thought to be Chosen together that day, but... only he had been Chosen. When he'd left, he'd kissed me passionately and said he'd write, or return for me.

But I had received only one letter from him months later. His name was now Lynx. He'd joined the Panther House of Nobles. He could not return for me, he was too busy with his new duties, but he wished me happiness and hoped I might join him one day.

I spoke in hushed tones, telling Auwei all of this.

The Panthers rarely take non-cat avatars, Birch, Auwei advised with a note of care in her voice.

I nodded. I was a spider and unlikely to rejoin my first love. I smiled sadly. "I know." I hadn't expected to be reunited with Lynx, at least not in his Noble House. The truth was, after he'd left, my feelings for him had cooled. He'd been kind and giving, but we'd both been a bit too hot-blooded and young. I was tempered now. Perhaps, if we met again, the spark would reignite, or perhaps not.

I hope you find a man who is everything you wish, Auwei said. *Or a woman. Or several men, or some mixed group. I'm open to anything.* I was a bit shocked by this. Despite group relationships being a known thing in Miraline, they weren't common.

"Have you...?" I asked tentatively, not really knowing what I was asking.

Later, Auwei whispered and I felt a bit of hesitation from her.

I nodded.

Still, Auwei whispered. *I hope you find someone to love, who loves you.*

"I'll worry about that once I'm Bonded with you. Until then, you're my one and only," I joked.

If that's the case, let's get back to work, yes? She crawled over the bed and onto a hand I lowered for her.

I found it odd that now that she had an avatar form, she couldn't float. She was... limited. Such a strange process the Lumani must go through, going from free-floating energy, then taking the limiting shape of an animal, then combining souls with a human.

"Why do you do this?" I asked. "Why go through all this trouble of limiting yourself, taking the shape of animals, and joining with humans. What do you get out of it?" I sort of knew the general story of the Lumani, that they had sought the experience of a physical existence, but I wanted to know Auwei's reasons.

That... is a long story, Auwei said.

"We've got lots of time."

True. In that case, let's start with a history lesson. Long ago, The Mistlands and your world did not cross over as strongly as they do now. They were two different worlds. We knew of yours, as we could see it through the Mists, but you knew nothing of ours. Then... one day, the worlds meshed and merged and people began to wander into the Mists. That's when we first met your kind and it's fair to say... both sides were quite fascinated with each other.

CHAPTER 5

Those first few of your kind who stepped into The Mistlands, especially those who stayed there and survived long enough, became the world's first mistweavers, able to draw on the power of my world even after returning to yours.

I shuddered at the mention of mistweavers. Tales of those ancient and powerful beings were still told to frighten children into behaving. Humans altered by the Mists, imbued with great power and cursed with madness. Spending too much time in The Mistlands did things to a human's mind.

The mistweavers had reshaped the continent. Some had ruled nations, others had destroyed them. Hence the Shattered Lands to the north. Thankfully, there were no mistweavers in the world today.

Yes, that was... something no one foresaw. A terrible time for your world and mine.

"For yours?" None of the tales mentioned any harm to The Mistlands.

Yes, some of the mistweavers learned ways to gain more power by consuming the spirits of The Mistlands.

I shuddered at the thought. "That's horrible."

Indeed. Auwei was silent for a moment. *But that time eventually passed. And later, some of my kind were intrigued by your world and wished to see it. But... our experience of the physical world is limited. Everything is energy to us. We don't see or hear in the same way as humans, and we cannot touch, taste, or smell. So, the first bargains and Bondings were made. It was a difficult experience for both parties, but in the end, the Lumani obtained the experiences of your world that they sought. Yet... when those first True-Bonded hosts died, their Lumani, though powerful in their own right were limited once again. When they returned to tell of their experiences, many of my kind were fascinated and wished to Bond as well.*

Auwei was silent for a long time after that. She seemed agitated, crawling around my bed and up the wall, then across the ceiling. She even spun a strand of spider-silk and lowered herself from the ceiling back down to the bed.

This form is really quite fascinating, Birch. I think you'll like it once we Bond.

"You're stalling," I said. "Is this difficult to talk about?"

Auwei sighed. *Yes.*

"Then we can stop for now."

No... I just needed a moment. The small form scampered up my calf and snuggled behind the knee of my folded leg. I would not have thought I'd ever want a spider snuggling up to any part of me, but with Auwei it was different. She had the rough form of a spider, but still had her cream-yellow glow and was warm and comforting to have near me.

My first True-Bonded... in those days they didn't change their names, did you know that?

"No."

They didn't take on the name of their avatar form. Her name was Woleia. Again, silence for a long moment. *She will*

always hold a special place in my heart. She was... brave, a
hunter, fearless when facing any beast of nature. She took the
form of a wolf. And... she was my first experience of your world. I
will always remember smelling my first rose, the sweetness of a
ripe peach, and the soft press of a kiss upon her lips.

I felt the heightened pleasure of these memories, trans-
mitted from Auwei. I too smelled a summer's rose, tasted
that peach, and felt the kiss. But there was more behind that
kiss. Emotions spilled into me, the warmth of love and the
wet heat of desire. For a moment, that overwhelmed me,
and I felt a thrill of arousal at the phantasmal press upon
my lips.

"Yes," I breathed softly as if responding to a lover's
caress.

Birch? I'm sorry, I didn't mean to... That was too much.

It had been. I shuddered as I slowly came down from the
rush of passion. I cleared my throat. "Ah... You were telling
me about Woleia?"

Auwei hesitated for a moment before continuing.
Perhaps we can talk more about Woleia another time.

I felt the depth of intimacy she was dealing with. There
was a lot more to Woleia's story I guessed, but I wouldn't
push. I let Auwei continue at her own pace and discretion.
You'd asked why I do this and what I get out of it. A sigh.
Humans tend to think of us Lumani as being powerful mystical
beings. And... I suppose we are when compared with humans, but
our power is quite limited, in this world at least. In the Mists,
everything is powerful, so... it's different. Our real power in this
world comes from our ability to Bond with humans and make
both sides stronger.

She remained silent for a long time before continuing.
When she did, her voice was hushed in my mind. *We... it*
hurts to lose a Bonded companion. Yet the joy we get from being

with one far outweighs the loss we feel when they're gone. It's like... being in love. I know you've only had one experience with that, but I've had many. My previous True-Bonded have loved... and been broken hearted. It's amazing, the power love gives you, the height of joy and contentment. Her voice soared for a moment before becoming sedate once again. *And when it's gone, it feels like the world has ended.*

A determined strength filled her. *Yet... I'd rather have loved and had my heart broken, then never have loved at all. And it's the same with Bonding. I am always devastated when my True-Bonded dies. Yet, the joy of Bonding with another will always draw me back to Choose someone like you, Birch.* Auwei giggled. *Or should I call you: Legs?*

"Spirits, no, please."

You brought it upon yourself.

"I know." I sighed. "But the fun and games are over. Tomorrow I need to focus on us, and Bonding."

I have faith.

I wished I did. I put on a smile and tried to feel strong and determined for Auwei, but doubt squirmed within me. If I wasn't able to Bond with Auwei I'd be sent back to my previous life.

That fear manifested in my dreams that night: living a life filled with a thousand mundane horrors, everything reminding me how worthless I was.

Suffice to say, I didn't sleep well.

CHAPTER 6

A KNOCK ON MY DOOR STARTLED ME AWAKE.

I sat up. "Yes?" I said before I fully understood what was happening.

"Breakfast, m'lady," came a girl's voice I didn't recognize from the other side of my door.

"Thanks!" I called, then flopped back into bed. A faint rim of light silhouetted my curtains. It was easy enough, from the bed, to lift a corner of the curtain and see a sliver of the sky. It was overcast and only barely light out, grey and gloomy. What an auspicious start to my time at Silverveil.

You'll want to make sure you get a good breakfast, Auwei said. *There's a lot to do. These days will feel very long and full. I'm sorry, I didn't think to let you know I could wake you whenever you like in the mornings. If you want time before breakfast tomorrow, to get ready, I can give you that.*

"Get ready?" I asked. I groaned as I pushed myself up to sit once again, then slid my legs over the side of the bed. My new dress was a bit rumpled; I'd slept in it. I tried futilely, to smooth it out. "And do what?"

Some of my previous True-Bonded liked to take baths or

showers in the mornings and do their hair or even put on some cosmetics.

Cosmetics? I'd never owned any. Also... "What's a shower?" I knew what a rain shower was, but I didn't know how a person could have one every morning.

There are facilities here where you can bathe, but also, you can have warm water pour over you in a consistent stream, called a shower. It's quite lovely.

"Perhaps I'll try one this evening. But no, I don't need to get ready, just wake me in time for breakfast." I rose and left my room. It seemed most of the other Chosen here had woken earlier as the great hall was full when I got there. I took some scraps of what food was left on the buffet and found an open spot at a table.

Still half asleep, I hadn't paid much attention to where I sat.

"Oh... hello," said a curious voice from beside me. "You're... ah... Legs... aren't you?" the young man's voice broke awkwardly.

With a mouth stuffed with warm bacon, I looked up to see I'd taken a seat amidst a group of boys. They stared at me with eyes full of... hunger, and not for the food in front of them. I'd never felt this *objectified*, and I was more than a little unnerved.

I blushed, suddenly wondering how I looked. I hadn't bothered with the looking glass in my closet. I usually had a rather frumpy tousle of hair in the mornings. *Spirits!*

Still, I tried to put on a winning smile. The boy next to me, the one who'd spoken, was small and slight with tanned skin and a tangled mess of light brown hair. Yet it was his eyes which caught my attention: soft brown eyes, so deep and curious and caring. His was a tender soul, I could tell instantly.

"Yeah... Legs, that's me," I said after finishing my bacon. "My actual name is Birch though."

"She's out of your league, Pebble!" one of the other boys called over. Instantly the one next to me — Pebble, an unfortunate name — blushed and shrunk into himself. "I'm Creek," the other boy said. He was across the table from me, head and shoulders taller than most of the boys here. A scruff of a beard grew on his chin, and his face was hard, eyes dark brown. I could tell instantly he was another charmer, like Oak, sure of himself and ready for action. All the boys at the table seemed to defer to him.

"I wish they'd let you keep that dress from yesterday," Creek said with a wink and a grin.

"Lady Kitsune had a conniption when she saw it," I said in response. "It's probably been burned by now. Hope you got a good look yesterday."

"I did," Creek said low and soft. "And if you ever want to show me... more..." He left the invitation hanging.

Yeah... no, sorry buddy.

Not your type? Auwei asked, but seemed to know the answer already.

Definitely not. I turned to Pebble, the smaller young man next to me. There was something about him, something in those eyes. *But him... maybe.*

Ah, yes, I see now.

I looked at Creek and decided to shut down any offers, from him or any other boys. "I'm not here to flirt or fulfill any boyish fantasies. I'm here to Bond with my Lumani, then test to become a Noble. Got it?" I stared down Creek, then each of the others in turn.

To be fair, you were the one strutting around like a peacock yesterday. Did your parents never teach you about the conse-

quences of your actions? Despite her words, Auwei was giggling.

They did, yes. I just don't often think that far ahead. I wanted to have fun yesterday, make an... interesting first impression. I only realized after the fact that I hadn't vocalized those words. I usually spoke to Auwei out loud, but it seemed, when not thinking about it — or perhaps when knowing I might be overheard — I'd inherently used an "inside" voice.

You're learning. Good, Auwei said. *And you definitely made one Pits of an impression on these boys yesterday. Also, in case you hadn't noticed, I think you've made some enemies among the girls.*

Enemies? Other than Cedar?

Over there to your left, two tables down.

I looked. A group of girls was staring daggers at me.

Auwei said: *A lot of Noble Houses intermarry, and they would have told their children to be scouting possible mates at Silverveil. But right now, you're sort of hogging all the guys.*

Trust me, I'm more than willing to share.

That may be true, but currently half the guys in this room only have eyes for you. And those girls are seeing the same thing. You may be making that speech a lot over the next little while.

Oh.

I hurriedly finished my breakfast and excused myself, noting how many pairs of eyes, male and female, followed me. It seemed in my short time here I'd made a lot of sort-of-friends and definite-enemies.

I rushed back to my room, hoping to have a moment alone, but was surprised to find a small, elderly woman waiting for me.

"Take off the dress," she said with a sniff. "So's I can measure you."

Oh... right... seamstress. Still, I was a little taken aback by her forward manner. It took me a moment of standing there dumb before I began to unbutton the dress. I was then subjected to various indignities as the old woman poked and prodded and measured.

"Thank the Spirits you've already got a woman's figure. I hate making girls' dresses, especially at this age, when they're likely to grow out of them in a month. If'n you don't mind a bit of advice from an old woman, you're a little too straight and thin. Eat more lamb and pork, put a little meat on ya. It'll help with childbirth and..." She chuckled. "All the bits that get you with child to begin with."

I was fairly certain I blushed down to my toes at that.

She was finished soon enough and left. I dressed again and decided to get some air before morning classes. I went out behind the girl's dorm and climbed the stairs to a lookout tower to gaze out over the wall. Fog blanketed the rolling hills beyond and a chill breeze swept over the high plateau on which Silverveil was situated. Given the dark clouds sitting low over everything, I had a feeling it would rain soon.

Auwei perched on my shoulder, silent.

Prompted by the seamstress's comments I asked Auwei. "Have you ever had kids?" Here, with no one around I felt comfortable voicing my words again.

Yes. I've been a mother five times and a father once.

"What's the big deal?" I wasn't sure I wanted kids.

She sighed. *It's hard to explain. And just so we're clear, it is up to you, and I'll be well if you decide not to have any. I'll say this much. Raising children is the hardest, most grueling, and exhausting thing I've ever done, but also the most rewarding, the most joyful. Yet, you can have a very full life without them as well, I've done that three times and been quite happy.*

"Ah..." That hadn't really answered anything.

If you don't want kids, what do you want? Auwei asked.

"That again?" I said, deflecting. I still didn't have a good answer for the question she'd asked during The Choosing.

Auwei chuckled. *It wasn't a test. I'm just curious. I Chose you because I sensed a fire within you, a strength of spirit which seems to come and go. I think, once you know what it is you truly want in life, you'll have that fire within you all the time. I would love to help you find that.*

I sighed. She was right, but I still didn't know. "I'll figure it out," I murmured and promised myself I'd do some thinking on it.

A bell rang for first classes, and I hurried down from my perch to join my group.

Oak winked at me as I arrived. I'd need to tell him what I'd told Creek.

Cedar glared at me.

Lady Kitsune either didn't see any of this or ignored it.

The six of us and our instructor met where we had the day before, but once we were all there, Lady Kitsune moved us away from the other groups to one side of the main gates. "From now on, we'll meet here when doing our group work." Kitsune was all business.

The next bit she seemed to have memorized. "There is no one way to Bond with your Lumani," Lady Kitsune began. "But over the many years that the Bondings have been happening we've learned several things that help. Exercise clears the mind. Similarly, meditation, whether moving or still, can help you center yourself and connect with your Lumani."

She pursed her lips, as if somehow what she suggested so far should be enough, and any further options were less desirable. "Yet, it may not be a clear mind or still soul that one needs to Bond. What seems to hold true is that a True-

Bonding often happens when one is doing an activity that speaks deeply to them and their Lumani. This could be swimming or solving complex problems. It could be writing a letter to a loved one or an act of creativity: painting or singing and such. It could even be doing something dangerous or exciting like engaging in combat, but I don't recommend that. There are many ways, and what you need to figure out is what will work best for you."

"*Many* ways?" Oak said with a grin. "Care to elaborate?" His sidelong look at me made it clear he hoped there was one way in particular which he and I might try.

"Ah, yes, well. Some Chosen in the past have engaged in various... activities, which are not recommended, but have been known to cause a True-Bond."

"Like sex?" Oak said plainly. Then he looked at me and smiled. Oh yes, we needed to have "the conversation" very soon indeed.

Lady Kitsune glared at him, tight lipped, but nodded. Her entire demeanor making it clear what she thought of that as an option.

"I've heard of Bonding happening while a person was playing pranks on another Chosen." This from Poplar. "Is that true?"

"It is." And again, Lady Kitsune did not elaborate. "You must find what works for you, BUT!" She raised a rigid finger. "Do not engage in such activities. We will follow a set course of classes and exercises which have been known to work in most cases. Only *if* that doesn't work *might* we consider other options."

"Got it," Oak said, but his grin was saying he was certain he knew what would work for him.

I shook my head.

And so began a morning of calisthenics and various

other ways to work our bodies and minds and "open our souls" to the Bonding.

By lunch I was already tired and mentally drained. The food helped to pick me up a little, but I was still somewhat off for the afternoon. As Auwei had warned, I was quite exhausted by the end of my first full day at Silverveil.

It rained that afternoon, but then the clouds cleared. After dinner I was ready for a bath and my bed. Still, I lingered outside, climbing that lookout tower from earlier, to watch the sunset.

That's where Pebble found me.

CHAPTER 7

I saw him coming from the corner of my eye, tentative and hesitant. He paused at the base of the stairs up to the tower, but then, after a moment, something seemed to solidify in him and he marched up the steps to me.

"Ah... Birch?" At least he wasn't calling me Legs. "I... I just wanted to apologize for how my table treated you at breakfast today."

He was apologizing? He hadn't done anything wrong. He'd been a gentleman. It was Creek and the other boys who'd been a little too forward. I looked over at Pebble. He was... well scrawny was the best word to describe his build. I doubted many girls here would look twice at him. Yet, once again something in his eyes caught my attention, a firm but tender determination. Something about it matched what I felt in my soul, my drive to become a Noble.

"Why are you apologizing for them?" I asked, curious.

He looked away, clearly self-conscious. "I just... don't think women should be treated that way."

I smiled. Yup, I liked this one. "How should they be treated?"

"With respect and honor, as an equal." Those soft brown eyes flashed up to look at me for the briefest of moments before looking away. "You are beautiful, yes, but I've learned that looks don't mean much. It's how a person treats another person that counts."

He was right. And he was being very respectful at the moment, which made me like him all the more. I pushed off from the railing and went to him. A finger under his chin lifted his face as I leaned down and gave him a soft, chaste kiss upon — what turned out to be — supple and pleasant lips. "Thank you," I breathed afterward. But I also felt the need to let him know that I still didn't want anything with any man right now. "When this is all done and we're both Bonded, come and find me."

He blushed a rather stunning shade of crimson, edging on violet, and nodded, seemingly unable to speak. I returned to the railing and Pebble left without another word.

When I heard steps on the stairs a moment later, I thought he'd returned, but I turned to see Oak approaching.

"Someone in the Rock class has already Bonded," he said, as he came to lean on the railing next to me, very close.

I'd noticed a bit of a hubbub and a carriage being prepared as I'd made my way to this spot.

"Truly?"

He nodded. "For some, it happens quickly." He turned, leaning his back against the low wall. "How are you feeling?"

"Tired, I just want a bath and a bed."

He quirked a grin at the mention of a bath, but since the girls' and boys' baths were nowhere near each other, the image in his mind wasn't going to happen.

I sighed. "I'm really not up for anything this evening, Oak; sorry."

He nodded. "Got it." There was a tightness to his voice. And with that, he left. Though, halfway down the stairs, he turned back. "And that walk, once I've found my avatar?"

I had said maybe to that earlier, but now...

You only live once, Auwei said. Then she giggled. *But I'll regret your mistakes for eternity.*

I laughed a little at that, but she was right. I couldn't help but feel that being with him would be a mistake. Though I couldn't say exactly why just yet.

"No, Oak, sorry," I said firmly.

His lips went tight and he gave a sharp nod. "Tease," he hissed. "You can go to The Pits for all I care!" Then he left in a huff.

And in that moment, I knew what it was about him that didn't sit right with me: he wouldn't take "no" for an answer. I had made no commitment to him, so it should have been a simple thing to accept, but he already thought I was his. No woman should be treated that way. I much preferred Pebble's approach to women.

Once the sun had set, I made my way down to the baths. A basement had been dug out beneath the common area and was accessible by a stairway from both wings of the dorm. The heavy fieldstone walls were dry and warm to the touch. There was some mystical power at work here. I didn't care to know the details, but Auwei informed me.

In some cases — in perhaps a quarter of True-Bonded? — the power that combines human and Lumani can produce powers beyond an avatar's abilities. For those with a particularly strong spirit, strange new powers can emerge. These are more like the powers the mistweavers held, though, generally far more limited in depth and variety. The baths of Silverveil were created by a

True-Bonded with such gifts, about a hundred years ago. They possessed power over the elements. Her voice was hushed and reverent within me.

The ground was dug out from under the dorms without disturbing a soul, stones were gathered and fitted perfectly for the walls, then imbued with a pleasant warmth to keep the bathing area warm and dry. The baths and showers are fed from a large steel tank of water, which fills itself perpetually, gathering moisture from the air outside. The waters are warmed as they are piped to their location and once a bather is finished, their dirty water drains away to the soil outside of the building. It's really quite fascinating.

It did sound interesting, but I was too tired to care. I decided to try a shower since I got the feeling Auwei loved them. I stepped over to the small stall and opened the door to a narrow, segmented area. The outer area held towels and had hooks for clothes. I closed and locked the outer door, took off my dress, hung it up, and stepped into the second area.

The steam from the shower will help to get those wrinkles out of your dress. You probably shouldn't sleep in it again tonight.

"Yup, sure," I said, staring at the odd bits of metal protruding from the wall. "So...?"

The thing with the holes at the top is where the water comes from. Don't look directly at it or you'll get water in your eyes. The lever at the bottom has three settings: warm, hot, and very hot. If you turn it to the first...

I did, and pleasantly warm waters poured out onto me. "Ohhhhhh," I sighed out heavily, leaning both arms against the stone wall, just letting the waters flow over me.

See? Auwei seemed to sigh with me.

"Yup, I get it now."

Curious, I flipped the bottom lever to its second setting

and the water grew warmer, like a perfectly hot, but drinkable cup of tea, only... on the outside. I gave another heavy sigh.

"The only trouble is, I just want to sit right now. I'm not sure how long I can stand here."

Auwei's tiny legs tickled as she climbed onto my foot, working hard not to get washed down the drain, which she wouldn't, she was too large.

Here, she said tenderly.

An odd revitalizing warmth flowed into me from Auwei. It wasn't much, but it roused me enough that I no longer felt faint.

I can't give much. I'll be able to give more once we're Bonded, when my life energies will be one with yours.

I felt revived enough to wash myself. I found a bar of scented soap and began to clean my body. I was filthy. After the soap I took an abrasive scrubber to my skin, leaving it red and raw. I thought that was it, but Auwei pointed out a large bowl in an alcove of the shower. *That's a special soap for your hair; try it.*

I did, scooping some of the gooey liquid into my hand, then rubbing it through my hair. Seeing some of the dirt washing down the drain from that, I proceeded to do the rest of my long locks.

"Do you care about my hair, our hair?" I asked, curious. "Is there a length or style you like?"

I'm good with whatever you want. I've had all styles and lengths. I love the feel and weight of a long fall of hair and how it covers me, but I also like the weightless freedom and versatility of a short cut. One of the men to whom I was Bonded eventually went bald. That was a new experience, but not as much to my liking.

"That shouldn't be a problem," I said with a laugh. I'd

have to figure out what I wanted. Dove had said she'd cut her hair back to just below her ears once she started taking more martial training at Pegasus House after she'd become a Noble. I couldn't quite imagine hair that short.

I finished with my hair and just stood under the hot water for a time, soaking it all in.

Finally, I turned the water off and grabbed a towel to dry myself. I'd seen some girls wearing the long towels — wrapped around them — back to their rooms. I didn't think I'd want to do that, but then... I looked at the dress I'd slept in the previous night.

Nodding to myself I wrapped the towel around me.

Almost as daring as your previous dress, Auwei teased.

It was wide enough that it covered me just a tad lower on my thighs. I laughed. "I think that's the most revealing I've ever been and probably ever will be."

Auwei chuckled. *We'll see.*

I didn't know what that meant, and didn't ask.

I turned the shower back on and washed the dress, giving it a good once over, then wrung it out and headed back to my room.

I hung the dress in the narrow closet, leaving the door open to help it dry. I was about to remove the towel, when I heard a commotion outside my window.

Curious, I snuffed out my candle lantern so my room matched the darkness outside, then pushed aside my curtain.

It took a moment for my mind to catch up with what my eyes were seeing. Pebble was running back and forth, trying to escape from three other, larger boys, one of whom was Oak. It looked like Oak had chased Pebble into the long alley between the dorm and the admin building, where two others had been waiting for them. Now the three larger boys were closing in on Pebble, backing him up against the admin building.

My fury rose. I couldn't abide a bully. Even back in Miraline, I'd often put myself in the way of those who'd tormented smaller kids. It had earned me a lot of bruises... before I'd learned how to hit back.

I opened my window and jumped out to help Pebble.

Even before I got there, the boys started throwing punches. Pebble looked terrified and clearly didn't know how to fight... but he was very adept at dodging, nimble and quick, evading their fists.

I reached the first young man, grabbed his shoulder and spun him around, landing a solid punch on his nose. My fist stung, but I followed up quickly with another hit to his jaw, turning his head and dropping him.

Now I had their attention.

And only then, as Oak, Pebble, and the other boy stared at me... did I remember I was only wearing a towel.

Bloody Pits! Too late to do anything about that now. Hopefully it distracted them, so I could end this.

Ah, yeah, they're boys, you're plenty distracting, Auwei noted.

"Legs?" Oak blinked in surprise, his gaze alternating between staring at my legs and the tops of my breasts showing above the towel.

I stepped over to the unknown boy and swept his feet out from under him. He fell.

"Run!" I hissed to Pebble, who now had a clear line of escape. He did, and he was fast.

"Bloody bones," Oak swore and looked at Pebble, then me, then his two friends on the ground, then back to me. "You love him that much, do you?"

What?

He must have seen you kiss Pebble earlier, Auwei said.

Oh... but...

To a rival boy, that would be enough to assume love.

Spirits! Why are boys so stupid?

I could see it now, Oak's jealousy. But he didn't go after Pebble, instead he reached for me... well, actually he reached for the towel.

Pervert.

Just as he got one hand on the spot where the towel was tucked in over my breasts, I punched him in the nose; stunning him.

He released me and stumbled back a step.

The guy on the ground near me grabbed for a leg, but I kicked him off, then kicked his face. Pebble was away, and now it was time for me to leave. I wasn't sure I could take on all three of these boys together.

Oak grabbed me again, his hand around my left wrist. He pulled me close. Lust hazed his words as he whispered, "Maybe I'll just take—"

I kneed him in the groin, then elbowed his shoulder as he doubled over.

I tried to run, but the first boy I'd attacked was up by then and managed to grab my towel. I quickly undid it and let him have it.

"Spirits!" one of them breathed as I sprinted the short distance back to my window... completely naked. I was up and back in my room quickly, shutting the window, closing the curtains, and breathing heavily. I doubted they'd try to get in here. One shout from me and they'd be in deep trouble.

"Well," I said between huffs of breath. "That was fun."

Was it? You liked that? Auwei asked.

I had. There was a part of me that just loved putting brutes in their place. "Yup."

Interesting... Auwei said. *Very interesting.*

I just hoped Pebble had gotten away and would find some place to hide from the others.

I was too energized to sleep, so I paced my room for a moment.

I knew there was something truly audacious about you, Auwei said. There was a confidence in her voice, a resolute I-made-the-right-choice sort of tone. *You felt so... alive, when you were out there, your spirit shining bright, it was amazing!*

Was it?

Yes, Birch. I think I've figured out one thing you want, even if you haven't.

Oh?

You want to put bullies in their place.

Yeah, I did. *True.* I'd have to think on that a bit more.

Then, in my pacing, I caught a glimpse of myself in the long looking glass. Right... I was still naked. I'd blown out the candle earlier, so the only light in the room was Auwei's faint glow. Still, I didn't need to see my reflection to know what was there, I'd seen it enough times before.

Tumbling curls of brown hair framed an oval face with a weak chin, and russet brown eyes. Nothing special there, though I did like my cute button nose and full lips. My shoulders were just a little too square, not the elegant slope of a lady. My arms were thick and strong from all the physical play — and occasional fights — as a child. I was a bit straight through the body with not much of a curve at waist or hips. Legs were sturdy and strong as well, though a bit leaner looking since I'd shot up in height over the last two years or so.

Honestly, I didn't really know what boys saw in me.

Yeah, I had long legs, but other girls my age had a lot more curves. I was far from the most beautiful woman out there.

What do you see in the mirror, I'm curious? Auwei asked.

"A girl who—" I cut myself off then sighed with a faint chuckle. "Yeah, that's the problem. I don't know whether I'm a girl or a woman. A part of me still wants to run and play and be free, but I also want to be... important and help this nation." Another sigh. "I can't decide if I'm a tall awkward girl, with too much of a figure, or an awkward woman with not enough of one."

Auwei gave the sense of a nod, bobbing a little bit. *Want to know what I see?* She went on, not waiting for my answer. *A beautiful and athletic young woman with so much potential in body, mind and spirit, to become whatever she wants to become.* My mother had said something like that the night before The Choosing. *I think you've just shown how much drive you have to follow your heart and your passions.*

"Thanks, Auwei." That meant a lot to me.

I slept fairly well that night, with pleasant dreams of knocking down arrogant bullies.

CHAPTER 8

THE WEEKS WORE AWAY. THE CHOSEN BEGAN TO BOND AND leave Silverveil. By the end of the first month, roughly half of the sixty or so Chosen had left.

Pebble was still around, though I hadn't seen much of him. When I had, he'd been keeping close to a young woman, someone from his group, I think. I didn't know much more than that.

Oak had avoided me after that night, though he'd taken to glaring at me like Cedar did. I think he and Cedar eventually hooked up, probably connecting over their mutual hatred of me. But then they'd Bonded with their Lumani and left.

I still hadn't Bonded, and it worried me to no end.

Of my group, four remained: myself, the quiet Maple, the shy and giggly Poplar, and the stoically determined Ash. We were all working hard, but the feeling in the group was the same... a questioning: why not us? Why not yet?

Then finally the day came when I was to go into the Mists. Generally, this was done either as a reward to those who Bonded early or as a boost for those who hadn't

Bonded yet. The five of us, my group and Lady Kitsune, walked for most of the morning to get there. First over a long ridge, then through rolling forested hills, then... to the thicker forests where the Mists hung heavy amidst the stout trunks of ancient trees.

"You will go in on your own, your guide will be your Lumani. Listen to them and heed their words. The Mistlands can be dangerous to unbonded humans." Lady Kitsune's tone gave no room for argument.

We spaced ourselves out, perhaps a dozen feet between us, then entered the Mists. One step into the heavy fog and I couldn't see the others, or much of anything. Occasionally, a thick tree trunk would appear, the Mists so dense I wouldn't see it until it was right next to me. Even then the trees seemed ephemeral. I tried touching one and had the oddest experience.

"I can reach into the tree," I whispered. This realm was made for whispers.

That's because it's not really there. It exists in your world, but you're in my world now and it's more a shadow of reality. You can walk right through that tree if you like.

I tried. It was unnerving, feeling it around me, but not stopping me. I didn't do that again.

"What did Lady Kitsune mean about The Mistlands being dangerous to humans? I thought all the spirits here were... friendly, like you."

Auwei sighed. *None of the beings here will hurt you... on purpose. But some of them are so anathema to physical life that they may... drain your essence. There are beings here, so foreign to your mind — and you so foreign to theirs — that they might feast on your life force and kill you, but think it nothing more than... as if you came upon a stream for a refreshing drink of water.*

"Oh." That was just a little terrifying.

But I'm with you, so I'll make sure that doesn't happen.

"Good." Slightly less terrified now.

What do you feel here? Auwei asked.

"Scared now," I said as a bit of a joke, though that was more truthful than I wanted to admit.

I mean physically.

"Oh... ah..." I stopped my wandering and closed my eyes to focus on my senses. It was odd. The fog against my skin felt like a breath of cool air. It didn't feel wet, like normal mist. "It feels cold but strangely dry." It only occurred to me then — and I couldn't help but blurt it out — that, "This isn't really mist!"

No.

"What is it?"

That defies explanation. It simply is. This is what my world is like. We never had a name for it until we met humans. You named it The Mists or The Mistlands, but we just think of it as home. This is our sky and earth, our water and plants. It is everything. Auwei giggled. *Want to know something truly astounding? You're not standing on anything.*

I opened my eyes and looked down. I could barely see my feet, so thick were the Mists. And below my feet, there were the faint hints of a forest floor, a few leaves, on which I was standing.

Just like that tree, the ground isn't real. Your mind is assuming you need to be on the ground because you always have been. But you can sink into the ground and be fine... or even fly.

"Fly?" That sounded fun. "I'd like to try that."

Auwei sighed. *Then do it. Though some of your kind find it hard to comprehend not being earthbound and are unable to fly. I can't tell you what to do or how to do it, since it's natural for me.*

I closed my eyes again and lifted my leg as if I was

walking up a set of stairs. It was the easiest thing I could think of. It took a couple of tries before my foot stopped where I expected it to. Then I simply mounted that set of stairs, higher and higher. Some part of my mind knew there was nothing there, but as long as I assumed there was, it felt firm beneath me.

Well done, Auwei said with genuine praise in her voice. *You did that far quicker than any of my hosts before.*

I tried to picture a light and fluffy cloud of a bed before me. I reached out, making sure I could feel it, then fell forward onto it and... floated. I caused the made-up bed to float around, here and there, back and forth, as I lay upon it.

You have a vivid imagination, Birch. No one I've known has done that before.

"Now, if only I could do the mystical thing that would Bond us. I'm even in a mystical land, literally *The Mist-ical* land, and yet... oh..." I'd flown through something cold that sent a shiver down my spine. "What was that?"

You flew through a sprite. They were very confused. Luckily, they're not the dangerous ones.

Still, it had felt quite uncomfortable and awkward.

"I think I'm done flying for now." But then I wondered... "Where's the ground?"

There is no ground here, remember?

The image of falling forever flashed into my head and suddenly my "bed of clouds" dissipated.

I fell.

"Auwei!" I called, as I tumbled head over heels through the Mists.

Even though she couldn't float in spider form in my world, she had been floating beside me here in the Mists. Now she flashed down and under me and I slowed, then stopped. I didn't know what she was doing. She had no physical form with which to catch me, but I felt a sort of warm pressure on my back.

Relax, set your feet down, you can have ground beneath you whenever you like. Perhaps I should have phrased it that way.

"Perhaps," I said, righting myself and visualizing ground beneath my feet. And there it was, solid enough to stand on, though I saw nothing in truth. "How did you catch me?"

I have more power here in my world. I can... exude a sort of force, which has presence in the Mists... It's hard to explain.

I was just happy she'd done it.

"I... think I'm done in the Mists, if that's well with you?"

It is, yes. I'm glad you got to see my home. Just... imagine yourself walking out of the Mists back into your world. Take two or three steps and...

"Oh!" I gasped as I did indeed walk right out of the Mists. "I thought I was farther from the edge than that."

Distance is like the Mists themselves, ephemeral. You travel more by thought than physical motion. Now you can see why we were so fascinated with your world. It was so vast and... weighty.

"I guess it would seem that way, wouldn't it?"

"Perhaps," Lady Kitsune said in a scolding tone. "If you spoke to your Lumani in your head and through your spirit, you'd Bond with them sooner?"

I blinked at her. Poplar was also nearby, looking a little awed and terrified.

I spoke with Auwei in my head all the time when I wasn't alone. I just... preferred to use my voice, but... Kitsune was right. If we were supposed to be Bonded, two in one body, then I'd have to get used to speaking to Auwei internally.

"Thank you," I said with a solemn nod to Lady Kitsune. "You're right."

She seemed a bit taken aback at my formal and apologetic tone. Then she nodded and that was that.

When Ash came out of the Mists, she wore a beatific smile, eyes shining... and her Lumani was nowhere to be seen. It took me a second to understand, but Lady Kitsune knew immediately. "You Bonded? Good."

Ash nodded, still seeming a little stunned. "I feel... whole," she said, then her grin grew.

Maple took a while to return, but he hadn't Bonded.

We walked back to Silverveil in various moods. Ash seemed light as air. Poplar was still trembling. Maple just seemed confused, while I was disheartened. Yet another of my companions had Bonded, and even though I'd been to the most mystical place in the world, I had not.

Don't give up. You have two months left, Auwei said cheerily.

But by the end of the second month, we still hadn't Bonded.

CHAPTER 9

A CURIOUS THING HAPPENED AT THE START OF THE THIRD month. Our existing groups were dissolved and remade with new instructors. Less than a dozen Chosen remained at Silverveil. Poplar and I were the only ones left in our original group.

They always do this, just to shake things up for those who remain, Auwei explained.

My new instructor was a dashing man in his prime, named Crown, with the avatar of a Crowned Eagle. I'd heard some of the girls talking excitedly about him in the past, and up close, I could see why. He was handsome, with an air of vitality about him.

Poplar and I were merged with the two remaining members of the Stone group: Pebble, and the young woman I'd seen him with, whose name turned out to be Hearth. She was plump and curvy, and the only other twenty-year-old in our entire class at Silverveil.

My anxiety was spiking, and not just because I hadn't Bonded yet. There was another, very important reason for my stress. The Noble-House Tests were in two weeks. But, given travel time, I'd need to be Bonded soon if I wanted to make it to the capital. They purposefully put them before the end of the Silverveil Bonding period. It was a motivator. If I wanted to join a Noble House, I'd have to go through those tests, and they were only held once a year. If I didn't Bond until after those tests, I'd have to wait a whole year to try, and even then, I might not get in. I had one week, maybe less, to get my act together and Bond, but the more I worried about it, the further and further that goal seemed to stretch before me. I was, at the same time, very close and impossibly far from achieving it.

Crown grinned at all of us as we gathered together. "You've probably been working your asses off trying to Bond, so here's a new strategy, take the day off. Wander the campus, even out on the hills, or sleep or lounge in a bath, I don't care. I'm here if you have any questions, but take all that pent-up frustration you're feeling and just... let it go. No one ever Bonded through frustration. Take today, get your energy back, and redouble your efforts tomorrow."

The four of us stood there, dumbfounded.

"What are you waiting for? Go!" He made a shooing motion with his hands, still beaming happily. "Have fun for a day!" he called after us as we began to disperse.

Poplar slunk back to the dorm.

Pebble came to me, followed by Hearth. "What were you going to do?" he asked me. He was still quite tentative and reserved in voice and posture.

Hearth spoke up. "Like we could *relax*!" she said, sounding as frustrated as I felt.

"We have to try," I said. "Crown's right. No one ever Bonded out of frustration. Maybe we *do* need to give ourselves a break. It scares The Pits out of me, but I'll try anything right now."

Hearth looked at me, then shrugged. "What do you plan to do? A bath sounded good."

I looked over at Pebble to see if he'd say anything and I caught the bright red blush on his cheeks before he quickly turned away. Someone had just been thinking of Hearth and me in the baths. Poor awkward young man.

"I like walking, I think I'll go for a long walk... then maybe have that bath," I said. "You're both welcome to come with me." I was curious to hear how things had gone for Pebble... and to learn about Hearth.

They both nodded. Hearth said, "That sounds wonderful."

"But let's get out from behind these walls," I suggested and marched to the gates, then out onto the hills around Silverveil, the other two in my wake.

It was a gorgeous early summer's day. I took several long inhalations of the fresh, warm air and found the other two following suit. We walked in silence for a while before that started to feel awkward.

"How have you been, Pebble?" I asked.

"Good." His voice was soft. He didn't go on.

I sighed.

Hearth drew me aside a moment later. She spoke, voice hushed. "He probably wouldn't say it, but he's very grateful for what you did that night."

"You know?" I asked in a whisper.

She nodded. "I had been out for a walk and he nearly bowled me over as he'd run around our dorm. Then he... he just burst into tears and I held him. He cried in my arms for some time and then, once he could speak, asked if I knew of any place he could hide, he didn't want to go back to his dorm."

Spirits! That was awful. Would Oak and the others have

tracked him back to his room? Probably. I hadn't even thought of that.

"So, I... ah... I sort of took him to my room," Hearth admitted.

I raised a brow at that.

"Oh, it was nothing like that, I was just giving him a place to hide. And, well... he never left. A couple nights later, we sneaked into his room and grabbed his things and his mattress. He's been sleeping on my floor ever since. We tuck his mattress away under my bed during the day and I... I have to sneak him down to the baths in the middle of the night. It's been awkward for him, for both of us." She looked me right in the eye as she said, "but we're just friends, that's it, nothing more."

"Oh?" It wasn't like I had some claim on the young man. "I would understand if you *were* more," I whispered.

She smiled. "No... I think he's got feelings for *you*. He's just never liked anyone like that before and he's confused. I've tried to talk him through it, but he gets all flushed and awkward and..." She sighed. "Poor boy."

I had to agree. "Thanks for letting me know," I said. Then, trying to include Pebble again, I raised my voice to ask both of them: "What did you two use to do before... all this?" I asked.

We waited, but Pebble remained silent.

Hearth went first.

"I was the daughter of a baker," she said with just a hint of longing in her voice. "I used to sit on a thick carpet to one side of the baking ovens and watch my father and mother work. I loved the smell of fresh breads and pastries." She gave a self-deprecating laugh, patting her slightly rounded belly. "I... may have had a few too many." She gave a pleasant sigh, then a heartier laugh. "I don't regret it. Everything they made was delicious. And when I was old enough, I joined them, helped them. My older brother worked too, and we were told early on that only one of us would be allowed to partake in The Choosing. My brother went for two years but wasn't Chosen. Then I went for three years and was Chosen in my last year."

She looked at the small green-brown mottled glowing bear that ambled along beside her. "Seioa Chose me, and I was so happy that day." She reached down to pet the oddly colored fur.

Auwei hadn't grown much when she'd taken the avatar form, but she'd been a spider, so that wasn't too surprising. It seemed Seioa had grown considerably, now half as tall as Hearth. We'd be safe on these hills. Few things were likely to attack us with a bear as our companion.

"Still..." Hearth sighed again. "I do miss that warm oven and those tasty treats." She was silent for a long time after that.

I looked at Pebble, hoping Hearth's story would prompt him to open up. Yet, still, he took some time before he spoke. When he did, his voice was so soft I had trouble hearing him.

"My parents died when I was three."

Spirits! I knew what that was like, what that did to a child. Luckily the Clarks had taken me in.

"I went to live with my aunt, but... she died when I was seven."

Oh... Blessed Spirits! Wow.

"That's terrible, I'm so sorry Pebble," I said, heartfelt. I couldn't imagine how I'd feel if the Clarks had also passed while I'd still been young.

Hearth hummed an agreement. She even reached out and laid a hand on his shoulder. He looked at her, tears in his eyes. His Lumani's avatar was that of a tiny mouse, the white glowing form buried in pebble's tangled tousle of thick, light brown hair.

"After that, I was allowed to stay in my aunt's house, no one else claimed it. But I was young and didn't know how to take care of it. By the time I was ten, half the roof had caved in. I was hungry all the time." He looked at Hearth with these words, a bit of longing in his gaze. I guessed it wasn't for her so much as the warm and comfortable life she'd led.

"I had to beg or steal for food. When I was old enough to go to The Choosing, I did. Though I didn't know it was a thing until I was already seventeen." Only then did a hint of a smile find his lips. "That's where Haleia found me." He reached up and gently stroked the luminous fur of the mouse with one finger.

Wow, if he was seventeen, he was small for his age, but then, if he'd been living alone and starving, that might explain why he'd been so skinny. He'd been eating well for a couple months now, and was starting to fill out. There was a strength to his slight frame, and I had seen just how nimble he could be and how quickly he could run. He'd be a handsome man someday. Though, handsome or not, his eyes still drew me in. I could see in them his compassion and tenderness... and grit.

"I... I never thought I'd be Chosen." His brief elation fell into melancholy. "And now I may end up back on the streets." Haleia must have said something to him as he soon added, "I know, I know."

It was a bit odd to hear someone speaking out loud to their avatar.

My heart broke for the young man. "You'll Bond, I'm sure." Before he could comment with something negative, I kept going, "I know we're all feeling down right now, which is why Master Crown was right, we just need to enjoy today. We can worry about everything else tomorrow. Let's forget our worries, at least for the moment and—" I drew in a heady breath of the summer's air. "—just enjoy this beautiful day."

He smiled faintly and nodded. "What about you?" Pebble asked after a moment. I thought I heard just a hint more strength in his voice. "Who were you before?"

It was my turn for a sad, nostalgic smile. "My name was Sara, and I was the daughter of two scribes who worked at the Library of Miraline. Though, they weren't my parents in truth. My birth parents were merchants and... never returned from a trip east into Vauphan when I was four. We got word that their small caravan had been hit by bandits." I swallowed hard, a single tear in my eye. It had been so long ago, and yet still stung me.

"Friends of my family took me in. My best friend became my sister. She's now a Noble in House Pegasus. She's... frightfully smart. Her name is Dove."

"I've heard of her," Pebble said, sounding a bit surprised himself. "The grounds of House Pegasus weren't far from my aunt's house. They're pleasant and calm, and I used to sneak over the wall to sit on their lawns some days, when I needed a break from the city." Ah, so Pebble was from the capital, for which the nation was named: Elista. Most of the Noble Houses had their physical house there, including Pegasus. "They say she is going to remake the city, that she has plans to tear up the streets and add something called sewers."

That sounded like Dove, always with a project in her head.

"I hadn't heard that," I said. "But it sounds like her. Anyway, we grew up a bit wild and free, but well educated."

I sighed. "I'd always wanted to be Chosen but had to wait for my last year before Auwei found me."

And I'm very lucky I did.

Thank you, Auwei.

"Everyone thought you'd be the first to Bond," Hearth said.

I looked at her, shocked, and she only then seemed to realize she'd said it out loud.

She blushed a little. "Well, you were the first to find your avatar. All the girls thought you'd be gone in a week."

Really?

I'd thought they'd all hated me. "I... didn't think anyone else thought much of me."

"You made quite an impression that first day," Hearth said.

Pebble nearly choked, coughing a bit to cover it up.

"Well, other than that," I said. "I'd thought everyone had forgotten about that quickly and just... avoided me."

"Well, yes, some did. But many others were intimidated by you."

"By me?"

"I'm not sure why you're surprised. You're older and towered over most of them. And you'd found your avatar on the first day. All the boys seemed to have eyes for you. You were everything the girls wanted to be."

"Oh..." I said.

You never know what others think; hence, it's never that good to dwell on it. They don't matter in the end. Only you matter, as well as your friends and loved ones.

I nodded to that.

"It was all just a show, a joke," I said a bit softly. "A couple of the other girls, Cedar and River, had stolen my other dresses and—"

"Oh, I know, everyone knew. Everyone hated them for it. If they hadn't done that, then you'd never have stolen the attention of most of the boys. Those two weren't particularly popular either."

"Oh." There was so much I hadn't known about. "Was the attention of the boys really that much of a thing?"

Hearth stopped and stared up at me. I stopped too, and Pebble made a slow arc around to the other side of us, stopping. Hearth shook her head. "You... you have no clue, do you?"

Apparently, I didn't. "About what?"

I did tell you that many Noble Houses sent their boys and girls here to scout for a possible match, Auwei reminded me.

Oh, that.

"Silverveil is the place where young Nobles go to Bond, in more ways than one." Hearth seemed very shocked that I didn't know this. "Since people come from all over the nation, and any of them could be a Noble within a matter of months, everyone is on the prowl for who might be a good match. The boys are told to look for girls that are bright and beautiful and driven, and the girls are told to look for boys who are... well, pretty much the same."

She cleared her throat a little. "They're even told to dally a bit if they wish, but not to make any true commitments. The point is to pick out who they want to make alliances with later. You... you threw that whole process into chaos."

I smiled. Something about that appealed to me. I'd never known the Noble Houses were so... cutthroat and cunning, sending their youth out to make alliances for them. It seemed creepy to me. I was glad I'd messed up those plans.

"Suffice to say, if you become a Noble, you may receive several offers for marriage," Hearth said.

"Oh!" That shocked me.

What happens if someone from one Noble House marries someone from another Noble House? I asked Auwei. *Have you ever done that?*

Most marriages are within a Noble House. But when two Houses come together like that the couple gets to decide which House they would like to be a part of. They cannot remain in both.

Oh.

It is a way for some people to advance up into a more prestigious Noble House. Though I'll tell you now, more prestigious does not necessarily mean better or more generous, or anything of that sort.

That made sense.

I sighed. "I don't want any of that. I'm not here for a husband. I'm here to Bond, and yes I want to become a Noble, but... I..." Well, I didn't know if I'd want to "marry-up" or not. I guess it would depend on which Noble House I ended up in... and which man proposed.

I sighed again, running a hand through my hair, shaking my head.

"I need more fresh air," I said and turned, walking once more. With my long legs and swift stride, the others had to hurry to catch up. Once they did, I slowed a little to accommodate them.

"What do you two want to be?" Pebble asked, his voice so soft, I barely heard it. It took me a moment to register the question. By then Hearth was answering.

"I... I want to create a safe place. I want people to have a warm place to rest, and caring people around them, like I had growing up."

I nodded to that. Her bear avatar made more sense now.

She'd do whatever it took to protect those in need, like a mother bear did for her young.

"That would be nice," Pebble said. "What about you, Birch?"

Oh, this question again. I felt like I needed an answer now, more than any other time I'd been asked. Hearth's answer had been so clear and concise. I could almost picture it. Shouldn't I want something that clearly?

I took a moment to ponder my avatar: a spider. If Hearth's bear was indicative of her desires, then perhaps a spider was indicative of mine. But what did a spider want? To spin webs and scare people?

No... so then what?

People talked about "a web of lies" so did I want to deceive people?

No.

There were other sayings about being caught in a web...

Caught...

Oh, I felt that. Did you think of something? Auwei asked.

Maybe... it feels sort of right...?

I tried to sound confident as I said, "I want to catch people, bad people, doing bad things. I want to bring them to justice." Something about that resonated deeply within me.

"People like me?" Pebble whispered.

"What?" Had he done something wrong? Oh... he'd mentioned stealing, being a thief. "No, not like that. You were stealing to survive, that's different. I'm talking about people who are really hurting others. Like Oak and those two who attacked you that night. I can't abide that."

Auwei had said, that night, that she'd figured out more about me. But it wasn't until now that it sank in for me. I'd run in to face those three without a second thought. I really did want to punish those who harmed or threatened others.

Even as a child I'd stood up to bullies and reported things that weren't right to my parents. I'd gotten my share of black eyes for my trouble, but they'd been worth it. I'd done what I'd known was right in the moment.

"Besides," I said to reassure Pebble. "I don't think a Lumani would Choose someone who was truly bad."

Ah... well... Auwei's hesitancy surprised me.

What?

Not all Lumani are as benevolent as you might think. Remember all those Noble parents who sent their kids off to scout matches. They're all True-Bonded with Lumani. And some Nobles I've met have been... ah... well even more corrupt.

Truly? I thought—

It's not something we share openly, but... we Lumani start to take on some of your human characteristics after a while. It's one reason I'm a bit girlish and giggly. Others have acquired less desirable traits over time. When they Bond now, they seek humans like them, which only perpetuates and builds upon their nature. I've met some surprisingly vile True-Bonded. I wouldn't say it's common, but you should be aware such True-Bonded are out there. I don't sense anything like that from Pebble or Haleia though.

I was too shocked to reply. What sort of world would I be getting into, if I was chosen for a Noble House?

Auwei tried to assuage me. *Some Nobles may be corrupt, but really, most of the Noble Houses are good places.*

Most?

Well, ah... yeah. I could sense her discomfort. She'd dug herself a hole, and I wouldn't let her out of it. *Your sister's House, Pegasus, is quite lovely. Some of their members are a bit full of themselves, but I wouldn't say they're bad people. And*

Pterolycus House is a bit wild and dangerous, but never to inno-cent people. They protect our border in the north and need to be a bit fiercer in nature. Panther House are insular and can be a bit superior. There may be a few not-so-nice members there. Wyvern... well I know you idolize their leader, and Skyfire is a true soul, but some of her members are a bit... bloodthirsty. They, like Pterolycus are fierce protectors of the nation, but some like battle and killing a little too much. The same is true of Grizzly House, they have a ferociousness to them, but few would ever dare to use it anywhere other than to protect Elista. Tanuki and Porcupine Houses are generally good and wholesome Houses, open and friendly, though looked down on a little by some of the other Houses for their charitable work. She hesitated, pausing a moment. The only two she hadn't mentioned were the Royal House, Owl, and House Maverick.

What about the Royal House? I asked.

They are, strong and powerful...

What wasn't she saying? *But?*

But... they don't all want to use that power for the good of the nation. Some of them are a bit too power hungry. They'll stay in line as long as Queen Whitewing is in power, but I fear what may happen if she dies.

I was shocked.

I didn't know what to make of this. I'd thought the Royal House to be a strong and guiding influence over the nation, but if it was filled with selfish, power-hungry types, what would happen if the benevolent Whitewing stepped down? If she died, there would be a Council of Nobles, where the various House Leaders would choose a new Royal House and perhaps Owl might not be chosen. But if Whitewing stepped down then others from her House would rise to power. What then?

I asked Auwei.

I don't know.

Not what I wanted to hear.

And what about Maverick? I asked.

They're... odd. A House of misfits and outcasts. It began with a few Nobles who left their Houses, seeking a place to fit in. They found that together and founded a new House. Maverick has made itself a safe haven for anyone, but I truly don't know what it's like there. Not a House I've ever been a part of.

Ah.

Wow.

That was a lot to take in. My thoughts whirled and I walked in silence, not even hearing the conversation between the other two for a while. When I finally did tune in to their words once more, I guessed I hadn't missed too much.

"What do you want?" Hearth asked Pebble.

Pebble sighed. "I just want to get off the streets... find a real home."

Maverick would probably take someone like him, Auwei said softly. *I don't think he's got what it takes to make it in any of the other Houses, though.*

Would I?

I no longer knew where I might want to be placed. I'd always wanted to be in House Owl but now... I wasn't so sure. Pegasus sounded nice and that's where my sister was. Perhaps Pterolycus or Wyvern? I'd need to be fierce to fit in there, but I was passionate about protecting the nation, so maybe?

You'll do fine, wherever you end up, Auwei said reassuringly.

I hoped so.

The day drew on and eventually we all grew hungry. We made our way back to Silverveil but had missed lunch.

Hearth and Pebble waited in the shade of a tree, chatting, while I went looking for Crown. I hoped our instructor might be able to get us some food.

I found him in the great hall chatting with a few other instructors. He spotted me and nodded, breaking off his conversation and coming to me, a basket in hand. "I noticed you three weren't at lunch, so I put some things together for you," he said handing the basket over. "How was the walk?"

"Good. We learned a lot about each other."

His blue-eyed gaze caught mine for a long moment. "I think I'm going to let you take the lead with those two, if you're well with that."

"Oh? Why?"

"You took a natural leadership role with them. I'd like to nurture that." He shrugged. "We don't know much about how the Bonding happens so there isn't much I can really say, but I can help you to find out a bit more about yourself during this process."

"Oh, thank you," I said, a bit stunned.

He smiled and winked, turning away to return to the other instructors. I took the food out and we three had a quiet meal in the shade of the tree, while I pondered all the strange, scary, and surprising things I'd learned that morning.

Have faith, Auwei said to me. *Crown has faith in you. You should too.*

A leader?

That didn't seem like me at all, but... maybe?

CHAPTER 10

THE ATTACK CAME AT NIGHT.

My only warning was Auwei screaming into my head: *Birch, wake up, move!*

I snapped my eyes open, already moving to sit up when I saw the shadowy form over my bed, and the flash of a knife.

I shifted at the last minute and the knife slid along my right arm, just below the shoulder, instead of hammering into my chest.

Pits! What was happening?

I reacted without thinking, kicking out. I caught the person on the side of their leg, hard enough to shift them. They stumbled to one side as I rose from my bed in a fury. My experience with those bullies meant I knew how to throw a punch and the attacker was caught off guard when I slammed my fist into their nose.

They reeled back, hitting the wall. I kicked up between their legs. Man or woman, that would hurt. They grunted, bending forward, and I brought my knee up into their face. Their head snapped back with a crack and they slumped lifeless to the ground.

Bloody Pits!

I stood frozen for a long moment, in shock, not knowing what to do. I should run, or light a lamp, or check this person, but I did nothing as my mind reeled.

They were dead. I don't know how I knew, but I knew.

I'd killed a person.

But they'd been trying to kill me.

It was all too much. I had to do something or I'd collapse into a heap, overwhelmed. I had to keep moving, and I certainly didn't want to be here. My mind latched onto the idea that if I had been attacked, perhaps others in the dorm were in trouble. So, I crept to my door, which was open, and peered carefully out into the hallway. I saw no other movement in the shadows.

I sneaked out, creeping to Hearth's room, which was three doors down from mine on the other side of the hall. As I reached it, the door opened cautiously and Hearth peered out. I could see Pebble further back in the room, looking frightened.

"What's going on?" she whispered. "I thought I heard something."

Yeah, she'd probably heard me, fighting for my life. But as to what was happening? I had no clue.

Remain calm and we'll figure this out. Though even Auwei sounded a bit stunned.

Before I could come up with any coherent response to her question, Hearth's gaze focused on my arm. "You're bleeding!"

I am? Oh right, the cut on my arm. I'd been so agitated, the pain hadn't fully registered. Even now, it didn't seem that bad, it was bleeding, but the cut was shallow. I'd be fine for a while.

I can help with that. Auwei was over the spot a moment

later and spinning a thick web over the long slice, stopping the blood. It felt cool and slightly soothing.

"Ah, yeah, I know," I said finding my words again. "Someone attacked me. I don't know what's going on, but others might be in danger. I'm—" I'm going to do what? Go out and find trouble? That was a stupid idea. Facing a few bullies was different than fighting armed killers. I'd only survived in my room because of desperation and flailing limbs.

So, what would I do?

"You two stay here and bar the door. I'm going to find out what's going on." That sounded more reasonable than going to fight. I'd just... take a peek, nothing more. Perhaps go find an instructor. Yes, that was a wise course.

Hearth nodded and closed her door. I heard furniture being moved. Good, they were safe.

Just remember, Auwei said. *You only live once, but I'll regret your mistakes for eternity.*

She'd said that before as a bit of fun, but now it was a warning.

I crept to the end of the hall. Reaching the door to the outside, I hesitated, terrified. I'd take a quick look out into the yard before going any farther.

The door creaked as it opened, just an inch.

"Is she dead?" a harsh female voice asked. A shadow next to the door began to turn my way.

She...? As in me? Just me?

Dead... as in...

What The Pits was going on!

My heart thundered. I stifled a yelp as time seemed to slow. I had to get out of the way, but where? I panicked as something seemed to shatter inside. Everything became clearer, the dark hallway crisp in my vision. A great upwelling of energy and vitality sprung to life within me.

Jump! Auwei shouted. Her voice inside my mind had always sounded a bit distant, but in that instant, it became clear and close.

I leaped, but instead of launching myself back, I went up, and with far more ease and effect than expected. I put my hands out before I hit the ceiling with my head. When my hands touched the ceiling, they stuck. I didn't fully register this as I pulled my legs up after me. I was still in my nightdress with bare feet and I curled my body around to press my feet to the ceiling as well, crouching awkwardly. My feet stuck too.

Birch, we—

Not now! I hissed internally as a figure poked their head in through the door below.

"Arick?" the woman asked. She was masked, all in black, like the attacker in my room.

Another voice outside asked something, but their voice was low and I only heard "... happened?"

"I don't know. The door just opened on its own? Odd." The figure poking their head in looked carefully to either side, then slipped back out. I heard her say, "If he's not done soon, I'm going in."

Blackened bloody bones!

Not wanting to be here when they came in, I crawled away... on the ceiling.

Birch!

Not now, Auwei!

No, Birch, this is important, you're using my powers! We Bonded!

Some part of me was already quite aware that normal humans did not stick to ceilings. But I had more important things to think about. People were trying to kill me and I was freaking out. I had to get away.

Great... how does that help us? I asked.

Ah... I don't know yet, Auwei admitted.

Then be quiet and let me think!

I skittered to the far end of the hall and was about to open the door to the common room — from above — when all the hair on my body stood up and I felt the strangest sensation thrum through me. I was *hearing* people talk, very quietly, on the other side of the door. Only I wasn't hearing with my ears. The sound reverberated into my body through the thousands of standing hairs all over me.

At first, I couldn't decipher the noises I was taking in from this new sense, but I quickly adapted.

"...freaks me out."

"Yeah, I know. I can't believe we're working for her. She scares The Pits out of me."

"Hopefully this job will be over soon and we can..." I didn't need to hear any more to be both terrified and certain I couldn't go through *that* door.

I couldn't leave through the doors at either end of the halls. I probably should have gone back to my room and out the window, but that didn't occur to me in the moment. No, I could only think of the one other way out of this hall: the stairs down to the baths.

I crawled down the wall and back to the floor, slipping into the open archway to one side of the hall, and treading lightly down the stairs into the baths.

I don't know if you'll be able to get out this way, Auwei said sounding a bit desperate herself. *If they have guards on these doors, they're probably watching the other dorm as well.*

I gave a manic chuckle as an idea started forming in my mind. *I'm not going out. I'm going to stay down here.* Yup, I had a plan. It was a stupid plan and very crazy, but I couldn't think of anything else.

Oh? Auwei breathed, curious, then... *Oh!* As she found my thoughts on what I planned. *That's... interesting...*

You're being kind... My plan wasn't to run but to hide. And if they came looking for me. I'd be ready. I didn't know why I thought I could fight them, but I did.

The large, long bathing room was completely dark, but my body-hair, standing on end, seemed to catch every twitch of the air and I just knew where the walls were.

I moved with as much speed as I dared, first to a shower stall, grabbing the large bowl of liquid hair soap. I sneaked back out to the entrance, where the stairs ended, and dumped the bowl all over the last step and the area below that. It wasn't quite enough so I went to another stall and got its bowl, making that last step a slippery mess. I then did the same with the bottom step at the entrance from the other dorm. Then I went into each shower stall and turned them on to the highest heat setting, leaving all the doors open. Steam poured out, making the room very hot and humid as a thick fog clouded the area. In the last stall I grabbed the towel and the scrubbing brush from the stall before turning the hot water on. They weren't much as weapons, but they were something.

I moved into the far end of the room where the baths were located. There was a large common pool if girls wished to bathe together, and past that several smaller pools with half-walls around them for private bathing. I got more of the liquid hair soap and doused the area coming out from the showers, making a path straight to the large bath.

I wrapped the towel I'd taken around my left arm and tied it off as a bit of protection if I needed to deflect a blow. I held the body-scrubber like a knife, not knowing what I'd do with it, but I was ready.

I waited.

The room grew stifling hot, and the thick, wet heat began to steal my breath and sap my strength, but still I waited. My nightdress stuck to me like a second skin.

Then I heard it: soft voices approaching.

"...by surprise. Her window wasn't open so she's in here somewhere." That's when it occurred to me to have slipped out my window, but it seemed they might have been watching that too... so perhaps this had been the best plan.

I heard a very faint squelch, then a clipped cry and the sound of someone falling hard.

There were murmurs for a moment, then a clipped curse. "The bitch killed Farin!"

Ha! Take that!

Another voice... the female one from earlier, said: "First Arick, now this. She's a clever little bitch, resourceful. Watch out for the last step and the area beyond, it's covered in something slick."

There were more murmurings for a moment, then finally a strong call: "Come out, girl! We know you're in here. Come on out and I promise to make it a quick death, pain-less. But make this any more difficult for us and I'll skin you alive!" This from that female voice. She must be in charge.

What have I ever done? Why do they want to kill me?

I'm not the one to ask.

Spirits of the Mists, save us.

Auwei gave a nervous laugh. *I am a spirit of the mist and I can save you. When they come, leave the fighting to me, I'll take control. You may have fought bullies, but I've fought far worse.*

Worked for me.

Two sets of footfalls crept closer. The light from a single

lantern swayed and slowly illuminated more and more of the baths as they neared.

A foot appeared from the hall of showers about the same time as two hands, one with a lantern, the other with a knife.

The foot hit the floor and, as hoped, slid out from under the person. They slid forward just enough that when they placed their other foot down to steady themselves it was also in the shower hair-soap I'd put down. At the same time, I reached out and smacked the face I saw coming into view with the body-scrubber I'd acquired. The person fell back while sliding forward, crying out as they went over the edge into the large pool as hoped. The lantern fell from their hands and hit the floor to one side, rolling away, casting wild shadows around the room, but remaining lit.

"Bloody Pits!" the female voice cried out. She leaped around the corner, over the soapy floor and landed right in front of me, murder in her eyes. She held a long knife in one hand with her free hand open in front of her.

I felt Auwei take control, sensed her readiness. But even Auwei was fooled. We expected the woman to attack with the knife, but it was her open hand that snapped out. The base of her palm caught me in the nose. My head snapped back, then bounced off the stone wall behind me. Explosions of pain blossomed in the front and back of my head. Auwei raised my towel-wrapped left arm to block the knife attack I expected as a follow up, but instead the knife slid over my belly, cutting deep.

Pits! Auwei cursed, but then she moved with such speed and precision. Even with my eyes clamped shut, my new spider's sense gave me a good idea where the woman was and we kicked between her legs, hitting home.

She grunted.

Auwei swept my arm down and hit the woman's hand. I heard the knife clatter to the floor. That same hand of mine then surged up to punch the woman's face, my towel-wrapped fist barely hurting at all as it landed. At the same time my right hand was moving over my stomach. I didn't know what it was doing, but Auwei did. My body was producing great quantities of spider-silk... from... my belly-button? I gathered it quickly in my hand and pressed it over the wound on my stomach, helping to stop the blood flow.

I stepped forward, throwing myself bodily into the woman and knocking us both into the pool.

Warm water surged around me and far too much went in my mouth. I found the bottom of the pool with one foot and surged up, coughing out water, seeking air. I opened my eyes to see the woman righting herself in front of me, and the other man — who'd gone into the pool first — now wading over to me.

I've got this, Auwei said with a calm I certainly didn't feel.

My right hand reached down and pulled another quickly spun gob of spider-silk from me, splashing up to throw it in the man's face. It hit home, covering his eyes. He'd be occupied for a moment.

Then we ducked under the water, avoiding a punch from the woman. Going horizontal, my feet found the wall behind me and pushed off, launching me through the water to the woman. I hit her — head first — in the belly. She folded. Auwei quickly righted us, then dunked the woman's head under the water as we came up. The attacker had lost her footing and flailed, frantic, as I used every ounce of my weight to keep her under the water.

One of her fists caught my ribs hard enough that I'd probably bruise, but that was it. She struggled for a moment longer, then began to weaken and slow before going completely still.

Well... that was sickening. I'd killed three people tonight, and I hadn't liked any of it. My only solace was that they'd been trying to kill me. Yet it still made bile rise in my throat.

Releasing the woman's head, I turned. The man had managed to scratch some of the spider-silk off his face, enough to free one eye.

I needed to deal with him quickly. Even with the spider's silk — and my towel-wrapped left arm — over my gut, I was losing far too much blood, growing weak. The man saw it too, the growing dark-red cloud around me in the waters. He grinned, a nasty thing, and came at me slowly. He'd managed to find his knife, and the blade gleamed, flashing in the light of that remaining lantern.

"Hazra said you'd be trouble, but I don't think she foresaw any of this. You've killed Lyena there, and the others, but I think maybe all I need to do is wait and you'll be gone soon enough." That nasty grin grew.

My sight grew dim, blackness fading in around the edges. I didn't want to get close to him, not while he had that knife, but I'd have to do something.

That's when I saw the two shapes coming out from the shower hall behind him.

"No," I whispered, but there was no strength left in my voice.

The last thing I saw before I blacked out was Pebble and Hearth charging at the man in the pool.

CHAPTER 11

I WAS RATHER SURPRISED TO WAKE UP AT ALL, LET ALONE IN A comfortable bed.

I groaned as pain, more remembered than real, sank its teeth into my arm and stomach.

Don't worry, we survived and you're on the mend, Auwei said, sounding confident. *Now that we're Bonded, I'm only semi-aware while you're unconscious, but I know we've been healed a little and bandaged up.*

That sounded good, but I still felt like The Pits. I groaned again.

"Legs?" The voice was familiar.

I pulled my eyes open and rolled my head to the side, feeling groggy and exhausted.

Slowly my gaze focused on the woman sitting next to my bed. First, I saw a pristine white gown, hands folded neatly in her lap. I looked up the strong, slender figure to find features I knew better than my own: golden-blond hair, bright blue eyes, small mouth, slight nose, and a familiar head-tilt.

"Dove," I murmured, my voice sounding rough. My heart both leaped for joy and settled with ease.

"Hello, sister."

"When did you get here?"

"I flew from the capital as soon as I heard the news." The capital was hundreds of miles away. She must have seen my look of stunned awe. "Doves can fly great distances quickly when needed," she said with a smile. "And I had good reason to hurry."

I nodded, head moving against my pillow.

After a moment, as my mind slowly cleared, something... the first word she'd said returned to me. "You called me Legs." That seemed odd. "My name is Birch."

She shook her head slowly. "You're Bonded now. Your Silverveil name no longer applies, and I'm afraid, in your case, you don't get a say in your True-Bonded name. It was what everyone here was calling you when I arrived. For better or worse, you're Legs now, Sister." She couldn't quite repress her tight-lipped chuckle.

Oh... great.

There are worse names.

Like what?

One of my Hosts was known as Tit for her True-Bonded name. To clarify, her Bonded form was that of a great tit, a bird.

Oh... yes, that would be awkward, wouldn't it?

She... we got used to it after a while. Just like you and that dress, we owned it.

"Legs," I sounded out the name. Auwei was right. It wasn't the worst.

"I sense there is a story behind that name," Dove said with a grin.

"Yup, but that's for later." I was curious. "How long...?"

"Five days since the attack."

Five days!

We were... very hurt. A Lumani can lend a little energy to help their host heal, but it's not much. It's a good thing there was a physician present at Silverveil to tend to you. If not for them... things may have been much worse.

And I am very grateful for your presence, I said and meant it.

You're going to have to live with me now, for a long while, or so I hope.

Me too.

"Who...?" I asked, still limited in my energy. Yet she seemed to understand what I was asking.

Dove shrugged. "They don't know who was behind the attack or why they seemed to be targeting you. Though..." She pressed her lips as if she'd said too much.

"What?" There was something in her look which scared me. "Tell me, Dove."

She sighed. "The attackers were assassins from the borderlands." That wasn't the bad part. No, given how she still looked shaken, I was sure there was more. "It's believed they were working with... a mistweaver."

I instantly went cold and heard Auwei's internal gasp of horror and fear.

"No," I whispered. "That's impossible."

She nodded. "So we all thought. But..." Again, she pressed her lips together for a long moment. I wasn't sure I wanted to know more, so I didn't prompt her, but she spoke after a few deep breaths. "There were five assassins taken alive, but before they could speak or tell us anything, *something* killed them. Some otherworldly force, taking the shape of mists, suffocated them. There was nothing we could do."

Well, wasn't that just horrible.

Also… why in The Pits did a mistweaver want me dead?

This is bad. Auwei sounded more terrified than anytime I'd known her.

Bad? Yeah, I know, but why are you worried? You're immortal.

Auwei hesitated within me, as if unwilling to go on, then she told me the truth. *Yes, we Lumani are immortal. We're energy, and when our host dies, we live on. But… it's possible… for a Lumani to be killed by a mistweaver with enough strength.*

Oh!

Exactly.

Auwei and I stewed in our fear and horror.

Dove, clearly sensing our confusion and dread, laid a comforting hand on the side of my head, stroking my hair. "You're safe now," she said softly.

Ah… no. I was being hunted by a mistweaver. I'd never be safe, ever again! But I didn't say anything. I let her have her comforting words; hopefully they comforted her.

We stayed that way for some time, and I managed to rest, even if I couldn't sleep or truly relax. After a while, Dove said: "I'm going to stretch my legs… maybe my wings. And it's time for you to have something to eat. Also, there are some others who would like to see you, I think. I'll be back." She leaned down to kiss my forehead, then rose and left the small room.

Then, in came a short procession of people. Master Crown came first with a tray of food, setting it on the chair Dove had just vacated. Behind him were Hearth and Pebble, neither had their avatars visible. Had they Bonded? I hoped so.

"How are you doing?" Crown asked softly as he sat on the edge of the bed. He pressed his lips together and I sensed a healthy dose of shame coming from him. "I'm

sorry. I should have been able to stop this, or... something."
Then he forced a smile. "I'm just glad you're well."

"I am, thank you." I tried to smile and failed.

"And you're Bonded! I would not recommend that
method of Bonding to anyone, but I'm glad..." He trailed off.
"I'm glad."

I nodded.

He rose, turned to the other two and nodded to them,
then left. Pebble took Crown's place on the edge of my bed,
and Hearth took the tray of food and placed it on her lap as
she took the chair.

"Can you sit?" Hearth asked.

"I think so?" I still felt achy and exhausted, but I wanted
to show strength for these two. I started to rise, then fell
back, my stomach spasming with sharp pain. That wound
was still healing.

"Let me help," Hearth said, giving the tray to Pebble and
helping to lift me and shift me so I was sitting sideways on
the bed. She took my pillow and put it against the wall for
me to lean on. "There."

My head spun a little now that I was upright, but it
settled quickly enough. My stomach still stung, but Hearth
had been careful and the pain faded as long as I wasn't
moving too much. Just sitting here wasn't too bad.

Hearth took the chair again and Pebble handed me the
tray of food. There were salted strips of dried pork, slices of
plum, melon, and a few blackberries. There was also a thick
slice of bread and a cup half-filled with water. I started with
the bread, tearing off a few chunks to eat tentatively. They
went down well and only made me realize how hungry
I was.

The others spoke as I ate.

"We've Bonded," Hearth said with a sad, confused smile.

"Like you." She forced a big grin. "Not the way I would have chosen, but it worked." A sigh. "I'm Blackclaw now. Not the most feminine name, but it fits. And Pebble is now Silence."

I smiled and nodded at each of them in turn.

"We... ah... well, we were terrified after you came around that night. We barricaded the door and hid, like you said, but then... so much time passed. We had no clue what was going on." She looked to Pebble — now Silence — and he nodded, taking up the telling from there.

His voice was still quiet, but now possessed a clear and resolute quality, which made it easier to hear and understand. "I... I was terrified and I just wanted to be as small as I could and hide." He looked away, clearly ashamed, but Hearth — now Blackclaw, what a name — leaned forward and put a reassuring hand on his knee.

He swung his gaze to her and something passed between them.

He drew a long breath and spoke again. "I felt the Bond happen, then... almost instantly I took my avatar form. I was a tiny mouse. Since we were so uncertain and curious, I sneaked out to the door and peered underneath to see what was happening. Two people were working their way slowly down the hall. When they got to your room, one of them cursed viciously and they mentioned someone was dead. From how upset they were I didn't think it was you. But then they went looking for you. They gathered someone from the far end of the hall then made their way down to the baths. I ran back to tell Hearth... ah... I mean Blackclaw this. She was the one who wanted to follow after them. She's far braver than I am."

I didn't know about that. He'd been there, right beside Blackclaw, charging in at my attacker, before I'd blacked out.

"It takes far more bravery to help when you're terrified,

than it does when you're not," Blackclaw reassured him gently.

I agreed with that sentiment.

I had finished the bread and fruit and was moving on to the pork. I bit off a small chunk and sucked on it, savoring the salty, smokey goodness.

Blackclaw took up the telling. "I was terrified myself, but... I had to help. Something... shifted within me. I needed to protect, to defend, to help, and I think that's what caused my Bonding. When I heard what Silence said, we cleared away the barricade, as quietly as we could, and sneaked out." She drew in a long, steadying breath.

I could tell, even just retelling the events was frightening for her.

"We crept along slowly, keeping well behind them. We were just reaching the bottom of the stairs when we heard the fighting. Your trap there nearly got me too, if Silence hadn't caught me." She smiled at him. "He was sure-footed enough."

He smiled at that and blushed a little at the praise.

"Even then, we were both scared and cautious," continued Blackclaw. "So... we thought we'd arrived too late. You looked... horrible, just about to faint into the baths and drown. I rushed forward, throwing myself at that last man. I was very surprised to see Silence there next to me and between the two of us we managed to subdue him and rescue you." She chuckled. "I can apparently be... quite strong when I want to be."

"But she took a cut to her arm," Silence said, voice heavy with concern.

"Bears have tough hides," she said with a grin. "It wasn't that bad." She pulled up the short sleeve of her dress to show the long cut on her shoulder and upper arm, still an angry red, but scabbed over. She wore it like a badge of honor. She looked at the wound for a long moment then nodded to herself. "I hadn't been going to test for a Noble House before, but... I think I will now. I need to be out there, defending people."

"I'm going to test too," Silence said with quiet determination.

I'd lost track of time. "When is the test?" I asked around a mouthful of pork.

"A little over a week."

"A week? In the capital? We'll never get there in time." I didn't know the travel time exactly, but by carriage it would probably be a nine or ten day trip. A fast carriage could get us there quicker, but those specialty coaches were hard to come by.

Blackclaw smiled. "They've heard of what happened here and agreed to extend the tests over a few days if needed. They're also sending a fast carriage for us." That answered that. "The physician thinks you'll be fine by tomorrow and ready for the trip, and there'll be beds on the carriage to rest as well."

I nodded to that. Finished with my meal, I put the tray aside and gave each of these two a long look. "Thank you," I said from the depths of my heart. "You saved me. I will never be able to repay you for that."

Blackclaw grinned. "We're fast friends now. No need for repayment." She put a hand out and I took it. Silence reached out to put a hand on both of ours.

"Fast friends," he said stoically.

"Fast friends," I repeated.

You could have done far worse for your first friends as a True-Bonded, Auwei said with heartfelt joy.

Indeed.

They left after that, and Dove returned.

I rested again and found sleep, even as troubled as my mind was with visions of a mistweaver haunting me. I woke with a start several times during the night, and eventually found Dove curled up with me on the small bed. I slept well enough after that.

The next day I wore the finest dress that ancient seamstress had made for me, packing the others away; they were mine now. I said good-bye to Dove and kissed her on the cheek. She said she'd meet me in the capital — she'd be there long before we would — and a moment later, she veered into her Dove form and flew away.

"Your sister is beautiful," Blackclaw said staring after her.

Silence nodded, though his gaze seemed to shift from Dove to me and Blackclaw.

We boarded the specialty carriage and were soon off.

Experiencing a fast carriage first hand, I had to admit, they were quite a marvel. The passenger area was wide enough that the benches doubled as beds. Two additional beds could fold down above each bench as well, sleeping four passengers. The coach was also extra-long, with a small sleeping area in front of the passenger area for the second driver. The drivers would spell each other out, riding in turns. And special way-stations were set up at intervals to switch out the horses. This way the need to stop was much less frequent. The final amenity were special springs for the wheels, which minimized the bumps in the road, making the carriage seem to float along, soft and even.

We made it to the capital in six days, arriving the day before the tests were due to start.

And for the entire trip, I tried not to think about the mistweaver after me. Though... something had occurred to me during the passage. Something that last man had said as he'd come for me. My mind had hidden it away, buried in the trauma, but I recalled it in a dream one night, starting awake. He'd mentioned a name, probably the name of the mistweaver after me. It wasn't much, but it was something. I knew who my foe was, even if I didn't know why they were after me, nor how to defeat them.

Still, I knew their name, and that was something.

Their name was: Hazra.

CHAPTER 12

AND SO ENDED MY TIME AT SILVERVEIL. I WAS BONDED AND AT the capital for the Noble House Tests, but I was still ill-prepared for the many trials to come. I thought myself tempered, but I was still so naïve.

I'LL NEVER FORGET SEEING THE CAPITAL FOR THE FIRST TIME. The sight of the white marble buildings glistening in the summer sun took my breath away as I gazed out the carriage window. Descending from Elismount, a low ridge of hills north of the city, I could see nearly all of the sprawling, sparkling city, which nestled into a wide, long curve of the Elis River. And after we had passed through the gates on to the city streets — paved with flat, square stones, perfectly fitted, such that they gleamed as one smooth surface — I gawked at the height of the buildings, and the finery of those on the wide walkways on either side of the road.

Blackclaw and Silence laughed at my wide-eyed wonder.

I was feeling heartier and healthier after the restful trip.

We'd eaten well, thanks to a purse of funds my sister had given to us for the journey.

I was feeling almost cheerful, though the thought of Hazra the Mistweaver, darkened everything. Still, for a moment, as I'd come into the city, I'd forgotten about my trials and simply marveled at the metropolis.

I kept the curtains of the window open but sat back on the bench. I couldn't help the great grin on my face, which made the other two snicker all the harder.

"You have to take me to all the amazing places in the city," I said, a little breathless. "After we all pass the Noble Tests, of course."

"Won't we be whisked away to our various Houses?" Blackclaw asked.

None of us knew.

"I hope we all get into the same House," Silence said, hopefully.

That wasn't likely.

Auwei had explained how the tests worked during the trip. After a True-Bonded had displayed their talents, one or more Noble Houses *might* offer to take them. Only then did a True-Bonded get to *choose* from those Houses offered. If only one House made an offer, that was their choice.

You *could* decline an offer, of course, then test again the next year, but few did. Declining an offer meant you were rarely given an offer again. Nobody liked being snubbed. Still, we had a small chance of ending up together. I secretly hoped for that as well, but mostly, I was just bubbling over with excitement at being in the city and being Bonded and being so very close to my goal of joining a Noble House.

If I was chosen.

But even the possibility of not being chosen, couldn't dampen my spirits that sunny day.

The carriage took us right up to the front of a massive building, a high-end lodging house called The Golden Rose, and stopped under a covered carriage porch, where I hopped out and ran to my sister, who was there to greet us.

"This city is amazing!" I said as I embraced her. She was shorter and a bit slighter of build than I was, and I nearly knocked her over with my enthusiasm. "I can see why you love it here so much and haven't gone back to Miraline."

She extricated herself from my aggressive hug and smiled, though her face quickly fell. "I should return home. I've been so busy. How are Mother and Father?"

"The same. Still spending all day at the library, and now that neither of us is at home to go get them, they'll probably spend all night there too."

She laughed at that.

"In all of my wildest dreams, I never thought I'd be staying here." Silence's voice, from behind me, was filled with awe.

"It's the finest place in the city," Dove said in return. "I wouldn't have anything less for my sister and her friends, those who saved her life."

I put my arm around my sister so I was facing the others and nodded. "Exactly. And we'll all be Nobles ourselves after tomorrow and be able to pay her back."

"There is no need for that," she said with a laugh. "It's my pleasure and my treat. Come, this way." She led us in through the massive wooden doors — which moved silently, light as a feather — to the sprawling lobby. It wasn't a common room like I was used to in other inns and taverns. The space was mostly empty. Though there was what looked to be a small wine-bar to one side, with a comfortable sitting area not far from there. The far wall had a desk with a pristinely attired young woman behind it. Dove approached her.

"These are my friends. What rooms were prepared for them?"

"Three-seventeen through to three-nineteen." The young woman handed over three keys to Dove with a smile.

Dove turned to us. "This way." She led us to a large space to the left and behind the girl at the desk. A wide stairway led up in a squared spiral, but what caught my eye — and I'm sure the others' — was the steel latticework column which the stairs were built around. A square area perhaps ten feet to a side was surrounded by this strong, yet somehow also delicate-looking steel latticework, which went farther up than we could see. At the base, there seemed to be a cage within that column of steel and a man within, also immaculately attired. He called out to us as we approached. "Would you like to use the lift? What floor?"

Dove winked at us. "Three." And she entered the contraption beside the man.

We all tentatively entered, and a steel lattice-work door was closed behind us. The man then pulled a cord next to him in three long, slow pulls. Nothing happened.

"We need to wait for the command to reach the opera-tors," Dove said.

Then... we began to ascend through the column of steel.

Needless to say, the three of us who'd never seen or experienced anything like this, all gasped and suddenly clasped the brass bar which was conveniently placed at hip-height around three sides of the cage.

We passed one landing then slowly came to a stop at the third floor. The man in the cage opened the steel door with a smile and we exited, all a little breathless... except for Dove, who was grinning at the three of us.

"Marvelous invention, isn't it?" she said in breathless awe.

We were all a little speechless.

Dove laughed, a light and airy thing, and turned to lead us to our rooms.

"I'll let you rest for a bit, but if you'd like to meet me down in the lobby after the sixth bell, I know a place we can eat." She handed each of us our keys as we reached our rooms. I was the last and she clasped me in a quick hug. "Enjoy," she said before turning to leave.

I entered the room and gawked. This one room was half as large as the home I'd grown up in and many times larger than the small cell at Silverveil I'd known for the past few months.

A large sitting area dominated the center of the room: a low table surrounded by two long couches and four chairs. To the right of that was a bed that was easily twice the size of anything I'd ever slept in. To the left of the sitting area was a sunken portion of floor with a large porcelain tub that looked like it could easily fit two people. Massive closets occupied the inner wall to my right. Opposite that, along the far side of the room, was a massive bank of windows, the glass so clear I had to approach tentatively for fear I might fall through the openings. Two sets of curtains could be pulled across the wall of windows. One was sheer and gauzy, allowing for privacy while still letting in light. The other set was heavier, to block out the light.

And when I explored the room further, I found an indoor privy, complete with a cord you could pull which caused water to flow through it and wash everything away.

Amazing!

A knock sounded at my door, and I answered it to find Blackclaw and Silence standing there.

"It's too much space, we both felt a bit odd. Can we come in?" Blackclaw asked.

I nodded, still a bit overwhelmed myself. Blackclaw and Silence sat at one end of a long couch and I took the chair next to it, shifted to be a bit closer.

"I'm worried about tomorrow," Silence admitted. We hadn't talked a lot about the tests on our way here. Apparently, we were going to do so now.

CHAPTER 13

"So am I," I said. "In terms of my powers... I can sense things around me and walk on walls, that's not much to show off."

Don't forget your webbing, Auwei said

At the same time, Blackclaw asked, "Can't you also produce webbing?"

I grimaced. "From my belly-button, yes, but I'm not going to lift my skirts to do that. I suppose I could cut a slid in a dress, but..." I shrugged.

There are many different types of dresses and garments available here in the capital. I've seen some more daring designs with the midriff missing.

That was an option too. I wasn't sure how I felt about that. It seemed a bit risqué for me.

"I haven't even tried changing into my avatar yet," I added. "Not that a tiny spider would be that impressive."

"That is pretty much all I can do," Silence said, shaking his head. "And who will want a mouse in their Noble House?" He seemed to shrink in on himself. "I shouldn't have come."

"Pish-tosh!" Blackclaw said with a friendly slap to his shoulder. "Of course you should have come. I think you two will do well enough. Remember that not every avatar's shape or abilities are flashy and impressive. Just think of the queen. She's an owl. She hunts well at night. I'm sure night vision wasn't something she could even show to the Nobles when she was testing. Buck-up, you'll be chosen, I'm sure of it."

I smiled. The stout young woman had a way of making everything seem... possible and easy. Even Silence perked up a bit.

"Now," she went on, "Seioa is telling me there is at least one problem we can solve right now. Apparently, there are dresses that have some of the stomach area missing. Why don't we use some of your sister's funds and get you something nice for the tests?"

See? I told you.

For someone who'd shown a lot of leg on my first day at Silverveil — and now had a name for the rest of my life because of it — I was feeling very anxious about showing my belly to anyone. Still... maybe it would make me feel as powerful as I'd felt that first day at Silverveil. Sure, I'd been terrified, but I'd been claiming my body, my power. Perhaps I could do that again.

"There's a shop not far from here," Blackclaw said. "Perhaps we can all pick up something special to wear." She rose decisively.

I couldn't help but be carried away by her excitement. I rose, and Silence followed.

We left my room and took the stairs down. The afternoon was waning when we left, though the midsummer sun was still high in the west.

We found the shop with ease — guided by Seioa — and

entered. And so began a playful bit of shopping, looking for just the right thing for each of us to wear. The shop owners, an aging woman and her daughter, came to help us pick things out and fit them as needed.

Silence was the easiest to dress, a fine pair of black pants and a dark-blue linen shirt fit him well, and we purchased those.

Blackclaw struggled to find anything that would fit; she was an awkward size being a bit shorter but fuller of figure. Still, we found a dress that cinched under the bust and was easily hemmed up to fit her height. Silence blushed seeing her for the first time. The outfit certainly emphasized Blackclaw's bust, and she played that up, strutting around a bit.

Then came my turn. We found several dresses that met my criteria of missing a portion around the belly-button. Blackclaw made me try on all of them.

The first was an odd dress, hard to get into. It had a loop behind the neck, a front-piece over my bust, then two straps which went around the lower back and connected low on the hip for the skirt. It showed my stomach, yes, and the skirt was long, but it showed far too much of the rest of me, being backless and missing everything from below my bust to the tops of my hips in front. My face must have matched its flagrant red coloring, blushing furiously as I wore it to show to the other two. Silence's eyes went wide before he averted them.

Yeah, exactly.

You look beautiful. You have nothing to be ashamed of, Auwei said, supportive.

Thank you, but I won't be wearing this... ever... again.

That red dress was the most revealing of the three I'd chosen to try. The next had a small diamond-shaped cutout around the belly-button, and the top of the dress covered well, but the skirt was short, cut on a slant such that the left side came to mid-thigh, and the right to just below the knee. It also had a slit up the right side, and if I stood with my legs slightly apart, most of my right thigh was exposed. I couldn't decide if this was too much or not.

Blackclaw thought this one, a deep green, looked best on me and would serve to emphasize my name.

The last outfit was less of a dress and more a skirt and top. It was a lavish dark blue, with a long skirt, belted tight around my waist, just below my belly-button. That was fine. The top however, had a low-cut neckline and a high-cut under the bust. I kept wanting to pull it down to cover more, only to realize I'd still be showing so very much.

So the green dress it was.

My heart pounded just thinking of wearing it... and thinking of the tests tomorrow.

To get used to it, I wore the dress to dinner with my sister that night, who remarked on it with wide eyes; saying I looked amazing, but she was stunned I'd wear anything like it. I'd never been one for such things growing up.

I still wasn't.

But as the evening wore on, I began to get more comfortable with it. Perhaps I wouldn't turn beet red when I was presented before the Nobles tomorrow.

Spirits and Sprites, I was so nervous!

And when we returned to The Golden Rose, I found myself tossing and turning, unable to asleep. While I lay there, I recalled my words to Pebble — now Silence — from long ago: *When this is all done and we're both Bonded, come and find me.* I should talk to him. I didn't know how things would go after the tests tomorrow, but if we were chosen for different houses, we might not see each other much after that. If I was going to talk to him, I should do that now.

I didn't bother dressing, remaining in my nightdress as I padded along in bare feet, slipping from my room then down two doors to Silence's room. I knocked softly, hoping he was awake and would hear it.

I was about to knock again when he opened the door. Silence wore only a set of long, loose breeches, which made it easy to see the hard, flat muscle on his chest and stomach, no longer quite as scrawny as I'd once thought him.

His eyes went a bit wide. "Legs?"

"Can I come in? Can... we talk?"

He nodded and let me in, closing the door softly behind me. As I entered the room, I looked back. I couldn't hear him, but there he was, silent as a mouse. His new name suited him well. We curled up in two of the large padded chairs and he waited, while I tried to find words.

"After the tests tomorrow, we may be going our separate ways and... before that happened, I wanted to... I wanted to know how you felt... about me." Wow, I wasn't usually the one stumbling over my words, but that hadn't been easy to say.

He smiled softly and blushed, as he always seemed to do, but this time it wasn't as deep a red. He nodded. "I've been thinking about that too," he said. "I... your kiss was my first." I saw him look away for a moment a faint smile on his lips as he perhaps recalled the quick encounter.

"Back at Silverveil, Blackclaw talked to me about my feelings and... love." His voice grew quieter now, tighter. "Haleia tried to explain it to me too, but... I..." He sighed. "I don't know if I understand. I've lived such a secluded and sheltered life. Feelings like this are hard for me to express, hard to figure out. I don't know if I love you, but when I think about you, I feel... warm and happy and I... my body..."

"Yeah, I understand," I said to save him any awkward details.

As for how I felt about him?

How do I feel? What should I say?

Tell him the truth... about his eyes, Auwei said.

Yes, right.

"When I look into your eyes, I feel a connection with you, Silence."

"You do?"

I nodded. "Yes. I see all your tenderness and caring, but also a determination. I know you want to become more than you were and I'm determined to do the same. It's what I see in your eyes that drew me to you."

"Oh," he said, seeming surprised.

"If we are separated tomorrow... I will miss you, dearly," I said and meant it.

"I'll miss you too," he said, and his gaze finally found mine again. And there it was, that conviction in his soft brown eyes. "I don't know if any woman will ever find me... will ever look at me, like you do, Legs." He seemed to grow more confident in that moment, but trembled at the same time. He grew flushed again and nodded to himself then said, "I would... like to be with you, before we potentially go off to separate lives." The words came out in a rush. His face was beet red now. That couldn't have been easy to say, to ask for. He'd put himself out there and I admired his courage.

I smiled and reached across the space between us. He did the same and we clasped hot hands for a long moment before I whispered, "I'd like that too."

CHAPTER 14

I DIDN'T KNOW WHY I WAS SO NERVOUS. THIS WASN'T MY FIRST time... though I highly suspected, from everything he'd said, it would be Silence's.

This may not be your first love, but there is always a nervous excitement for... new love, Auwei said tenderly.

She was right. I was trembling and excited. My body felt warm and unsteady.

Don't worry about how you feel, just... feel it, enjoy it, Auwei said.

So I did. I opened myself up to this wild energy and suddenly sitting there felt so very wrong. I rose and, through our joined hands, brought Silence to his feet with me. He trembled, chest heaving with quick and heavy breaths.

We stepped in toward each other and he reached his free hand up to caress my cheek. I tilted my head slightly into that touch, resting my cheek in his hand. I closed my eyes, feeling the warm press of his palm.

He stepped closer, his chest brushing the silk of my nightdress, under which my nipples hardened, pressing back into him.

His hand on my cheek gave a slight pull. I let him draw my face closer, opening my eyes and seeing a turbulent fervor in his gaze, matching how I felt.

His lips were soft and tentative on mine. Our hot breath mingled as we tested and tasted with chaste kisses.

He released my other hand to slide that arm around me, pulling me closer, tight to him. Warmth pooled deep within me as I felt the hardness of his lean frame against mine, my entire body searingly sensitive. My breasts pressed to the flat plane of his chest through the sheer fabric of my gown. Every shift of our bodies sent thrills through me. I felt his arousal, the firm press of his erection low upon my abdomen, through two layers of cloth.

I put my arms around him, keeping him close. My mouth opened first, and I teased my tongue over his lips. When his mouth opened to mine, our floodgates released and we dove into each other with all the pent-up desire hammering through us.

My hands roamed his back, feeling his wiry muscle. His hot palms pressed over my nightdress, feeling every contour of my back, sides, and behind. One of his hands slipped down and began to bunch up my nightdress, pulling it up over calves and knees. And when he could slip a hand under, he stroked my thigh and cupped one firm cheek of my buttocks, pressing us closer still.

Our need became a bonfire, raging and unstoppable. I separated from him, grabbing one of his hands to pull him across the room to his bed. And there, I lifted off my shift and stood naked and unashamed before him. I wanted him to see all of me. And I wanted to see all of him.

He didn't blush; instead, his eyes were hungry as he took me in. He untied his breeches and let them fall away. His cock stood proud and tall before him, throbbing and firm. He was a beautiful man, covered in lean, firm muscle.

He stepped in again and kissed me, but this time one of his hands slid down between my legs. I moaned into his parted lips as he pressed upon my folds. I was already wet as his fingers explored me, thrilling me. With all the pent-up desire surging between us it wasn't long before I wanted more than just his fingers.

My lips moved to the side of his face and I whispered. "I want you, Silence." Then, I moved him, turning to push him down on the bed. He sat on the side of the bed and I straddled him. I was slow and careful, but also desperate with hurried need as I lowered myself upon him.

And when my loins ground down upon his, and I felt his fullness inside me, we both gasped with trembling pleasure.

His hands came up to cup my breasts as I began to move, hips swaying and grinding upon him.

We both overflowed with heated urgency. This was his first time and I knew he'd not last long. I could see his eyes and mouth go wide in the moment before he couldn't restrain himself any longer.

"Yes," I breathed, giving him permission, as I pulled myself closer to him. His lips touched my breast and I felt a moment of trembling pleasure as he gasped through his first release. He pulled me tight to him as he shuddered, his lips finding the tight bud of a nipple to suck and play as he surged within me. It was enough to send another thrill vibrating through me, mild but satisfying.

Then he released my breast as he gasped again. His eyes clenched shut, mouth open as he shook with convulsing bliss.

And when, finally, he'd finished and untensed, I pushed

him back to lie on the bed and laid myself down, pressed atop him, kissing him gently.

"I... I'm not done, I can—" I hushed his lips with a kiss. I didn't care. I'd felt desired, hot and intimate, and had even experienced a thrill or two. I hadn't expected him to be a master of himself his first time out.

"Thank you, Silence," I whispered above him, my brown hair falling around us like a veil. And I meant it. I was truly gratified at how he'd reacted to me. I felt sexy and wanted.

"Thank me later," he said and suddenly rolled us over.

I laughed at the playful turn of events. He drew himself out and we shifted, moving to lay fully upon the bed as he knelt between my legs. He reached down between us and I felt a spike of bliss as his fingers began to work. He grinned. "Haleia knows a thing or two about how to give you a bit more. I couldn't quite hear her over the pounding of my heart before, but now..."

And Haleia was a proficient instructor indeed, as Silence's deft fingers began sending thrill after thrill through me. I didn't care how I looked in that moment, though I must have been a sight, chest heaving with gasping breaths, eyes rolled back, then closed, lips whispering worshipful words.

I let out a cry of surprise when I felt more than just his fingers pressing against me. It seemed he was quickly ready for more. He lowered himself a little, pushing into me. His hands on my hips pulled me close, driving him deeper. Then his fingers were back to where they had been, now caught between us as he moved within me once again.

I'd been on the verge of an orgasm, and the welcome surprise of his fullness hard within me sent me headlong into a powerful release. My entire body tensed and flexed as I closed around him. He began to thrust, slow and steady, as his fingers continued to work wonders. The combination was driving me completely mad with bliss.

I grabbed the heavy blankets, balling them into my fists as tears of utter, amazed joy slipped from beneath my clenched shut eyes. I rode the waves of a perpetually building orgasm until his pace finally picked up. A second, body clenching orgasm pounded through me as Silence drove to his release. Clinging to each other, we merged in bliss, gasping and crying out.

We lay in a twitching pile for some time after that, sweaty, messy, and spent.

"Thank you, Haleia," I said, once I'd regained my breath enough to speak.

He laughed, and I joined him, feeling light and free and wonderful in that moment.

I stayed with Silence that night. I hadn't thought I'd sleep well the night before the tests, but in his arms, I found peace and slept far more soundly than I had in a long time.

In the morning, I slipped back to my room quickly to prepare, then the three of us made our way to the testing grounds along with about two dozen others.

This was it. My time to shine... hopefully.

CHAPTER 15

I SAT IN THE CIRCULAR THEATER, WATCHING THE TESTS BEFORE mine.

The Royal Elis Theatre was three levels of steep seating formed in a circle, with no seats on the northern side of the theater; which was dominated by the stage. The stage and rings were covered, but the center was open to the skies above. The stone yard would be for the "masses" who wished to stand — there was no seating down there — and see a show. Today, it was in that open center where those being tested performed.

The Noble House representatives — the leaders of the nine Houses each with their second-in-command standing behind them — sat on the stage, evaluating those coming before them. There were few in the kingdom who could not name these powerful figures.

First among them was Queen Whitewing of Owl House; the Royal House. Her second was Merlin, a slight and small woman with a very intense look. The queen herself was relaxed and resplendent in a gorgeous white, flowing gown.

Her long white-blond hair settled around her, icy-blue eyes intent on the tests.

Fang, leader of Pterolycus — or Winged-Wolf — House was a large and broadly built man, powerful and dark of complexion with sweeping black hair and dark eyes. His second — and if rumors were true, his lover — was a tall and also strongly built woman named Retriever. She had beautiful black hair, cut short, and golden eyes. Together the duo looked both proud and dangerous. Lady Kitsune, who'd trained me at Silverveil, was a member of that House.

Next was one of my idols, Lady Skyfire of Wyvern House. She had flame-red hair and burning yellow-orange eyes. Behind her was Drake, her second. A rare duo were they, both with dragonesque forms, the rarest of avatars. He was tall with well-cropped brown hair and eyes which were constantly in motion. He seemed to be looking everywhere, on watch.

Another beauty, was Lady Silvermane of House Pegasus. She was the queen's daughter, but had chosen to start her own House instead of joining her mother's. She looked much like the queen, with silver-blond hair and cold blue eyes. She was young for a House leader, but already had a House which rivaled or exceeded the others. Dove was lucky to have been chosen by her. Behind Silvermane was Lord Horn, a massive man with grey in his dark hair and steely eyes. He'd been Silvermane's bodyguard for years and had become her second within the House. A dangerous fellow if the tales were true. Mild-mannered most of the time, until his charge was threatened, then a vicious and fearsome protector.

Jaguar was the leader of Panther House. A lithe and lean man with an easy smile, but an aura of impending danger, ready to pounce. His second was Tabby, a bookish woman, tall but willowy, with soft brown hair and spectacles before her orange eyes.

The last four Houses I didn't care as much for, but I still knew the names of the leaders, though, not their seconds. The enigmatic Lady Tanuki of Tanuki House, with dark eyes and fair hair. The massive Lord Grizzly of Grizzly House, a mop of dark brown hair on his large head. Everything about him was... oversized and dangerous. Then there was Lord Spike of Porcupine House, an odd-looking fellow, rake thin, with a wide grin. Last was Lord Maverick of Maverick House. He was a large fellow as well, a bit rounded of muscle and with an easy-going nature, often talking to his second, a severe-looking woman who never replied.

"Would Legs and Auwei, spider avatar, please come to the testing grounds!" the herald called out. My heart leaped with excitement while my stomach held a cold ball of fear.

Don't worry, do what we practiced and planned. You can do this, Legs. Auwei's words of encouragement helped to calm me, but only a little.

"You can do this!" Blackclaw said as I rose.

I'd sat in the top tier as I'd wanted to make a special entrance.

I kicked off my shoes and jumped up onto the half-wall at the inner edge of the tier.

"Here!" I called out. I quickly touched my belly-button, then the pillar next to me, then... I began walking down the wall.

I'd made sure to sit next to one of the massive pillars that supported the inside ring, so I could walk down that, without having to jump over the gaps of the tiers below mine.

The trouble was... I was heavy. This was far different from when I'd crawled along the ceiling back at Silverveil.

I'd been on hands and feet then, supported. But walking down a wall without using my hands meant my upper body was sticking way out from the wall and it wanted to bend, pulled down. So, I walked — very carefully, making sure one foot was solidly placed before moving the other — down the wall, trembling not only with fear, but with the effort of my muscles straining to keep myself straight. When I finally reached the stone yard I was shaking violently from the effort, but I'd made it.

There were various strange objects around the testing yard, some large and awkward, some shaped like people, for the testees to use to demonstrate various abilities. I'd already demonstrated my primary ability: wall-walking. The only others I knew of so far were jumping and my spider silk. I had attached a piece of silk to the pillar up at the third level and grabbed that now, pulling myself up a little, demonstrating that I had the silk and how strong it was.

Letting myself down, I separated that strand, then put my hand over the small hole in my dress, quickly filling it with a ball of webbing. I threw the webbing at a human-shaped "dummy" in the yard. It hit low on the "man's" face, covering the mouth and nose and a bit of the neck.

"Bloody..." I whispered; eyes wide. It only occurred to me in that moment that such an attack could be fatal, if my opponent couldn't get the webbing off in time, they'd not be able to breathe. That is not what I had meant to show, only that I had the "web-throwing" attack.

Don't worry, you're doing very well, keep to the plan.

I shook violently, but I made my way back over to the edge of the inner ring and... leaped with all my might. I actually didn't know how far I could jump. I hadn't fully tested that. So I was just a little shocked — I may have let out a terrified scream — as I passed well up, out of the theater, to perhaps double or triple its height.

I flailed wildly as I then began to fall.

Don't worry, I'll catch us, Auwei said, sounding only slightly less terrified than I was.

We landed on the roof of the theater in a crouch, springing up to our feet.

"Oh!" I breathed. "I..." I hadn't thought I'd land so lightly.

It only makes sense that if we are able to jump that high we will be able to land from that height.

"Oh," I said again.

Or at least, that's what I was hoping. I caught Auwei's hint of relief. She hadn't been certain.

I'm glad you were right!

Me too.

As calmly as I could, I walked back down the inner pillar to my seat. Several people had risen, rushing to the edges of the inner ring to look up and seemed relieved to see I was well. I smiled and nodded to them. Returning to the half-wall where I'd started, I bowed to the Nobles.

Looking at the nine of them, most did not seem particularly impressed. But then... they hadn't for anyone else either.

I took my seat again and deflated into a puddle of anxiety induced tears.

"Are you well?" Blackclaw asked as her name was called.

I couldn't speak only nod weakly.

She smiled and rose, taking the stairs down to the yard.

Silence reached over and took one of my hands, squeezing it. "I think you did an amazing job," he said reassuringly.

I smiled at him too, but couldn't stop the shaking or the tears.

I missed Blackclaw and Silence's test as I slowly recovered from the anxiety of my own. The three of us were the last to be tested, since those who'd Bonded first were tested first.

Then... we were all called down to the yard. This was it, the moment the Nobles would pick their new House members. And again, it would go in order, so I would be close to last. I was so nervous I could barely stand; shaking and weak. Blackclaw supported me.

Cedar — now called Swan — was chosen for the Royal House. I was certain if we met again, I'd never hear the end of that. Oak — now Badger — was chosen for House Pterolycus. I hoped I wouldn't be anywhere near him. Creek — now Cougar — was selected by Panther House.

There were a few, perhaps five, who were not chosen. The silence after their name was called was deafening. And so... it came to me.

"Legs and Auwei, spider avatar!" the herald called out. The Heads of the Noble Houses, now all standing, were silent. No one rushed forward to claim me. I even saw Skyfire shake her head slowly. Lady Tanuki shuddered. Time stretched as the herald counted in his head the thirty seconds the Nobles would have to step forward and say... anything really.

"And—" the herald began. My heart constricted in that split second before... a voice cut him off.

"I'll take her!"

Maverick had stepped forward, that strapping body of his was apparently quick as well as strong. He grinned down at me. "The others may not want a spider in their House, but I think you've got potential."

Potential? I'd take that.

I had to reply and say whether or not I accepted his offer, but my heart was thundering and I couldn't speak. A part of me hoped that now that he'd stepped forward, others would as well... but that didn't happen.

"Say yes!" Blackclaw hissed at me.

"Yes!" I blurted.

And that was that. I'd committed myself now. I would be a Noble of the outcast and misfit House... Maverick.

Great.

Better than nothing, Auwei said, with the equivalent of a mental shrug.

And she was right, it was.

Maverick nodded and stepped back in line with a smile. I'd been his first pick of the day. I could practically hear Swan's derisive laughter.

I was so lost in my own world I didn't hear who chose Blackclaw, only that she said "Yes," and seemed excited. I blinked, turning to her.

"Who?" I asked.

"She's a bear," Silence said. "So, who do you think? Grizzly of course."

"Ah."

Then Silence himself was called. Again there was a long pause before Maverick stepped forward. "Come to my House, little mouse. We've a place for you!"

Silence blinked in surprise, then looked at me with a wide grin. "We're..."

"In the same House," I said, excited. "Say yes."

"Yes!"

Maverick stepped back.

That was it, the end of the Noble Tests... and all three of

us had been chosen; Silence and I were even in the same House!

We three looked at each other and suddenly were whooping and hollering — among some others who were doing the same — hugging and jumping and celebrating.

Our House Leaders came to us, telling us to take a night in the city — to celebrate and say good-bye to friends — and meet them tomorrow.

Maverick took Silence and I aside and gave us each a small, but heavy bag of coin. "There's only the basics in Grovner's Green, the town near Hedgewild, where you'll be going. So, buy what you will today, there's a lot more here of whatever you may need."

Blackclaw had a similar chat with Grizzly, then the three of us were running out of the theater, arm in arm in arm, elated beyond reason.

We'd made it.

We'd actually made it!

CHAPTER 16

AFTER A DAY OF SHOPPING AND SPENDING NEARLY ALL OF WHAT our new Lords had given us, we turned to celebration.

I drank more than I ever had that evening. Dove joined us for our party, temperate as ever, not drinking much, which was good, since none of the rest of us could remember how to get back to where we were staying.

I woke up the next morning with a splitting headache and a mouth that tasted like fuzzy dirt. Luckily Dove had stayed in my room, sleeping on a couch, and got me up and ready.

"You're a Noble now," she said once I was mostly returned to my senses. "You need to start acting like one." She grimaced. "There are some who take this charge lightly, spending their time gambling, drinking, or chasing men or women. I know you won't be like that. We are the leaders of this nation and need to be an example to others. Are you ready for this?"

I nodded. "No more drinking, ever... ever again."

She grinned. "I didn't say you had to stop drinking forever, just... maybe not that much all at once, yes?"

"Yes, definitely yes."

"Good."

She saw me to the lobby, where we waited for Blackclaw and Silence, who joined us shortly thereafter. Blackclaw looked little the worse for wear after the night of celebration. Silence looked as bad as I felt.

"Good-bye, sister. I love you, stay well," Dove said, embracing me.

"Love you too, sis," I said holding her for an extended moment. "Try to get home. They miss us... I think."

She nodded. "I'll try."

We held each other until it became awkward, then separated, nodding to each other, a few tears in our eyes. After that, the four of us went our separate ways. Well, Dove and Blackclaw went different ways, while Silence and I went another. The two of us paid a porter to carry our things. The man led a donkey with our bags and trunks — most of which had been purchased yesterday — on a cart behind it. Neither Silence nor I had had much before we'd come here, now we had... lots. Though I would eventually come to find out that what I thought of as lots was still a paltry amount compared to most Nobles.

"I wish I had a sister, or any family, like yours," Silence said softly.

"We have each other," I said with a wide smile. "And Maverick House will be our family now. Let's go meet them."

He beamed at that and we hurried to our meeting with Maverick.

The meeting place was to one side of the main carriage depot in Elista. We arrived to find Maverick leaning casually against the wall outside, thick arms crossed over his broad chest. He was a bull of a man —

which shouldn't have been surprising given his avatar —
with strong heavy shoulders and chest, arms packed with
rounded muscle, a fit and slender waist, and strong legs.
He wore a shirt with the sleeves ripped off, stained in a
few spots. His breeches were sturdy leather, his knee-high
boots, well worn. He had a mop of unkempt, thick brown
hair, some of which threatened to cover his eyes, while
most of the rest stood on end in cowlicks and curls. He
didn't seem to care. His brown eyes and easy smile were
welcoming on that broad and ruddy-red, leathery face
of his.

Next to him, in complete antithesis of his appearance
was his second, a woman of my height, slender and poised,
standing straight. She wore a simple, long dress, belted at
the waist, with full sleeves and a high neckline, conservative
and respectable. Her pale silvery-blue hair was pulled back
in a tight braid, which was then wrapped up in a bun
behind her head. She was immaculate and clean, her grey-
blue eyes sharp, small mouth pursed. It was she who spoke
as we drew near.

"I am Lady Crane," she said with clipped, clearly enun-
ciated words. "You know Lord Maverick."

He nodded and grinned.

"He will be staying in the city, while I escort you to your
new home in the south. I will explain everything you need
to know along the way, but we have a carriage to catch so, if
you are ready to depart, then let us do so."

She turned, fully expecting us to follow and we did. She
seemed a bit cold and harsh to me, very different from
Maverick.

The large man spoke as we passed him. "I may not be
home for a while, so I'll say it now. Welcome to House
Maverick." He grinned. "Do what Crane says and you'll do

well. She's in charge while I'm gone." Then he pushed off from the wall and ambled into the city.

"I don't think the two of them could be more different," Silence whispered to me.

I had to agree.

We were bustled into a regular carriage, with Crane sitting opposite the two of us, and she spoke again once we were underway. "The trip to Grovner's Green will take two days, and Hedgewild Manor — your new home — is another few hours out from the town. We will rest tonight in Elisford, then take a ferry across the river tomorrow and continue southward." She paused and looked intently at us, perhaps expecting questions, but we remained silent. She nodded. "You were given a small sum with which to purchase items while in the capital. I noticed you arrived with some bags and chests. Did you find what you needed?"

We nodded.

She smiled. "Quiet ones, are we? Good. I like the quiet ones. Listen to me and ignore the other gadabouts at the House, and you'll do well enough." Another pause, then, "Neither of you are the children of Nobles, are you?"

"No, miss," Silence said. "I... lived on the streets before I was Chosen."

Crane corrected him. "Please address me as 'Lady Crane.'"

"Yes, Lady Crane," Silence said.

She nodded to that. Oddly there wasn't any of the cynical repulsion other Nobles had had to Silence's low-born upbringing. If anything, I thought I saw just a hint of solace and sympathy in those cold blue eyes. Interesting. She was proper and stern, but not... superior.

She looked at me.

"I was the daughter of..." I trailed off. I shrugged. Might

as well tell her everything. "Of merchants, but they died when I was young and I went to live with friends, scribes at the Library of Miraline, Lady Crane."

She raised her brows. "Are you educated then?"

I nodded. "Yes, Lady Crane."

"Good." She passed an assessing look over both of us again, then proceeded. "You will find those at House Maverick come from... a wide variety of backgrounds. All are accepted and welcome. Remember you are now Lord Silence and Lady Legs." She pursed her lips after saying my name, I could almost read her thoughts: *Lady Legs? How vulgar a name.* Still, she forced a smile. "It will be up to you how formal you wish to be with your title. Some are less concerned with it than others."

"Like Maverick."

She grimaced. "Like *Lord* Maverick, yes." She shook her head. "The day I get him to fully accept his nobility and role as leader of our House will be the day I can finally rest." She seemed to realize she'd said too much and pursed her lips again, a habit.

"What questions do you have?" she asked.

"What... do we do... as Nobles?" Silence asked.

I could see the unasked questions on her lips: *You became a Noble without knowing what they did?* Still, she took the question in stride. "Nobles are the rulers and protectors of our fair nation of Elista." Her tone was that of a teacher. One I'd heard often from my parents.

"You will need to be educated, in case called upon to adjudicate civil disputes. You will also need to be able to fight in defense of the kingdom. House Maverick is tasked with protecting the south of the nation, which... is one of the easier assignments of all the Noble Houses since there are no southern neighbor nations, only the ocean. So, we fight off the occasional pirate, help towns hit by raiders, and otherwise keep the peace in the south. Occasionally the Royal House or the Council of Nobles will give us a special mission to complete. That... hasn't happened in a while."

Silence nodded.

For his benefit, I added, "The Council is made up of the leaders of all the Noble Houses, with the queen or king at their head."

"That is correct," Crane said. "Though some House Leaders defer their seat on the Council and rarely show up... like Lord Maverick."

My turn for a question. "What is it like at House Maverick?" The name of the manor had been mentioned a couple of times, but it hadn't stuck in my mind yet. "Hedgemaze Keep, was it?"

"Hedgewild Manor." She drew in a long breath and actually seemed to relax a little. "The grounds are amazing. Rolling fields and hills in all directions, with scattered woods and the Greyling Forest to the west. To the east — about a day's walk — is Dyrens Bay, with glistening clear blue waters. There are tenant farmers who work the lands around the estate, so we have a variety of fresh fruits and vegetables depending on the season. And separating the fields from each other and the estate grounds are many hedges of varying heights, which give the manor its name."

She paused for a breath. "The house has two wings, a central hall, and five towers. It's... in a bit of disrepair at the moment, though I'm doing my best to keep it up. There is only a small staff who tends to the place, since our funds are somewhat... limited. We are not as important a House as those in the capital or guarding the north and west." She sighed at that. "But we do what we can. Life is... interesting. I am hoping you two will not be a burden on the House as some of the other Nobles are." Another heavy sigh. "Lord Maverick takes in... all sorts."

I was beginning to wonder what our new Noble family was going to be like. It sounded like they were a wild bunch, barely kept in check by our current hostess. Which led me to my next question. "Who are the other Nobles in the House?"

Lady Crane nodded. "You'll meet them all soon enough." Still, she listed them off: "There is Lord Ant, Lord Jack, Lords Fennec and Foggy, who are brothers, then Lord Fin, and of course Lord Maverick. For the ladies, there is Lady Amber, Lady Tusk, Lady Sparrow, and Lady Princess. Please note, 'Princess' is her name not her title. She is *not* actually a princess, as much as she acts like one. There is also Lady Midnight, but you won't meet her. She's on an extended mission, something even I don't know about."

I would like to have said I couldn't wait to meet them, but given how Lady Crane spoke, I didn't quite know what I thought of the eclectic-sounding group.

The rest of the day, as we traveled, Lady Crane informed us of the various duties we'd have around the manor and gave a bit of a summary of the usual missions we might be called out upon.

The road followed the Elis River for most of the day. That night we stayed at Elisford, a village near a spot on the river where it widened out into a small lake and was fairly calm most of the time. It was a fishing village for the most part, but being on the main road, it had a respectable inn, in which we stayed for the night. Silence and I went for a walk along the river, to stretch our legs after the long ride that day. We held hands and talked freely, a deep bond forming between us.

The next morning, we and the carriage were carefully loaded onto a wide barge and ferried across the river.

The second day, as we traveled, the lands grew hilly and at some of the higher peaks, I could start to see the distant strip of glistening blue: the ocean, specifically Dyrens Bay. We reached Grovner's Green just after noon and had a meal there, before continuing to Hedgewild Manor, arriving late in the afternoon.

We pulled off the main road onto a long driveway bordered by low hedges. At the end of the drive, it circled around a central fountain. There was no covered carriage porch. Instead, wide steps led up to massive double doors in the middle of the central part of the manor. Two long wings came out from the main building, flanking the drive-yard. At the front of each was a tower, several levels higher than the three stories of the regular building.

From what I'd seen descending into this pleasant valley, the back ends of those two wings — stretching out behind the building — also had towers of the same height. At the center, right above the entranceway, stood a fifth tower, taller than all the others, with a dome of glass atop it. Dozens of evenly spaced, dark windows peered out from walls of grey stone, which were almost completely covered in ivy.

As we pulled into the yard and around the circular drive, I could see what Lady Crane had meant by "disrepair." The fountain at the center of the front yard wasn't working, it was dry and missing bits of the stonework. The house itself — though the ivy hid many faults — seemed to be crumbling; this was evidenced mostly by the small piles of stone and mortar in places at the base of the walls. As the carriage came to a stop, I could see the wide steps up to the door were missing small chunks here and there, and the double doors seemed to be mismatched, perhaps one was older, or of a different type of wood?

I stepped out and was surprised to see a large, strapping man approaching the carriage. I hadn't noticed him as we'd come around the drive. I'd thought the yard empty, so he gave me a bit of a fright, especially given his size. He was well over six feet tall and if I'd thought Maverick was muscular, this man made him seem scrawny. Yet he had a twinkle in his clear dark-brown eyes and a friendly smile on his lips. He was also shirtless, showing off his dark skin and a massive expanse of chest, not to mention the chiseled muscles down his stomach, which were... distracting.

He greeted us with: "Hello all, I'll grab your things, you go on in." He reached the back of the carriage in two long strides and unstrapped our trunks. He curled my trunk and Silence's easily under one arm and Lady Crane's larger trunk under the other, like they were nothing!

"Lord Ant!" Crane said, scolding. "We have staff for that! And put on a shirt!"

Lord...?

Ant...?

For some reason, I'd pictured Lord Ant as being small and skittish.

Ant laughed, a full and easy sound. "Why make them do it when it's so easy for me?" Another laugh. "And if you think my bare chest is bad, Jack's... in one of his moods."

I didn't understand that last bit, but it made Lady Crane pale. Then, she bristled, and the pallor disappeared.

"This way," she said and hurried us inside.

Silence opened the door for the two of us women, the vision of a gentleman. Inside was a long hallway, left to right, and another set of double doors across the hall from where we entered. Unlike the outside, this hall was immaculately clean and well preserved. I guessed this was Lady Crane's work, since the main entrance would need to make a good impression. She might not be able to patch every crumbling stone outside, but she could make this look good. Smooth tiles covered the floor in a patterned mosaic, and half-column stands held vases and other small items of note in even intervals down both sides of the hall. But that... was not what caught our attention as we entered.

"Hello ladies," said the fit and lean man who passed us in the hall. And I could tell he was fit and lean, with lithe, long muscles on that tall, slender frame... because he was stark naked. He winked a dark-brown eye at me — his hair a perfect fall of wavy, raven locks — and whispered, "Come see me later, and I'll give you a tour you'll not soon forget." Then his suave smile grew as he looked over at Crane. "And if you ever want to... unwind and let loose, I'll always be available, *Lady* Crane." The way he said *Lady* made it both an insult and a sexual invitation.

We all stood there blinking as he continued away from us down the long hall.

"That..." Lady Crane said, voice trembling with barely restrained rage. "Was Lord Jack."

I tore my gaze away from his tanned and perfect skin, blushing deeply as I turned back to the others.

"Let me guess," Silence said wryly. "His avatar is a jackass?"

Lady Crane made a noise I would have never thought to hear from her, a sort of half-snorting-half-choking sound. I think it was a restrained laugh. She regained herself a moment later.

"His avatar is a jackrabbit actually, but... you aren't far off otherwise." She drew in a long breath. "He may be a rather good fighter, but he's impossible to live with. I still can't believe Lord Maverick chose him." Another steadying breath. "Now, if you'll follow me."

We crossed to the other set of double doors. Through them, a large hall spread before us, longer left to right than across, but... the view across was stunning. Many windows let in the light from the south and gave a view of the garden courtyard beyond. "This is the great hall where you'll take your meals. Breakfast service starts promptly at seven."

After that, we were given a quick tour of the estate. It was H-shaped with the great hall and entrance corridor forming the middle, connecting piece. Down the long wings were many other rooms of various sizes. I quickly lost count and forgot the specific names for most. Then we came to the library at Hedgewild, which occupied three stories at the south end of the west wing. So many shelves and so many books. I'd seen more in the Library at Miraline... but no other place. This was the second largest collection of books, tomes, and scrolls I'd ever seen.

Then we were shown to our rooms. Our trunks were already waiting for us, brought by Lord Ant, no doubt.

"Dinner service will be in one hour at six sharp." Crane left us with that and marched away.

And that was it.

We'd arrived at our new home.

CHAPTER 17

S<small>ILENCE AND</small> I <small>ARRIVED FOR DINNER AT SIX, DRESSED IN OUR</small> finest, and ate with Lady Crane. However, none of the others in the House showed up. Lady Crane ate with a rigid silence that we didn't want to break, so we returned to our rooms after that. Well, Silence came to my room and we sat together on a long couch and talked.

"What do you think of all this?" he motioned to everything around us. My room, like his, was large. A massive four-poster bed dominated one side of the room, with a small sitting area on the other. Closets lined the inside wall and a bank of windows stretched all along the opposite side of the room. It was a lot like our suites at The Golden Rose, only a bit smaller and without the bathing area, though there was still a small water-closet and privy. I couldn't believe this was mine now... all mine. I said as much to Silence.

He laughed. "Yeah, I'm... overwhelmed. I went from a run-down shack to *this*. I think I'll get used to it though." He sighed. "Mostly I'm just glad to have you here with me." He put a hand on my thigh and I liked the warmth and feel of it.

I could feel his trepidation. I couldn't imagine what his life had been like before all this, nor how much of a change this must be for him.

I leaned over and kissed him lightly. "I'm happy I can be here for you. Just let me know if there is ever anything you need."

"I will, thank you, Legs." He grinned. "What did you think of Lord Ant and Lord Jack?" he asked.

"Ant is... big, and Jack is..." I shook my head I had no words. I laughed then. "Though, if they're indicative of the others, I think we'll be in for some more surprises."

"Yeah," Silence said, laughing with me.

We chatted idly about the house and a few other items before Silence kissed me lightly and rose. "I'm... heading to bed," he said.

I saw him out. I was glad he hadn't wanted to stay with me that night. Our encounter before the Noble's Test had been amazing, but... that had been when we thought we might not see each other again. Now, we knew we had time to get to know each other more, let our relationship grow and flourish. I honestly didn't know if I could say I loved him. I cared for him deeply and we shared a unique bond, but love...?

You'd know if I was in love, right Auwei? I asked.

Indeed I would, and you are right to think this is still... new. There is infatuation and connection, but true love, that usually takes time to blossom. I am happy you have found someone. Though I feel from you as if... you may want... more?

That was what I couldn't put my finger on. I liked Silence a lot, but some part of me didn't seem satisfied. And it wasn't that I wanted someone else, more like... one person just didn't seem like enough.

I've had hosts who entertained many lovers before. I think perhaps you may be like them. Something to think about, Auwei advised.

And think on it I did, as I fell asleep that night, though I reached no resolution.

Silence and I were in the great hall at seven sharp the next morning. Once again, it was only Lady Crane who we met there. But this time, after we'd eaten and she'd left, we stuck around and waited.

At half-past the eighth hour, a woman in a long, light robe entered the hall. Her head cocked to one side as she noticed us. She smiled and came over.

Silence averted his gaze. There were two things which probably caused his shamed blushing. The first was simply how the woman walked, a gliding, full-body movement which exuded grace and languid sexuality. The second was the robe itself, which, though opaque, was light enough that the morning light seemed to shine through it, silhouetting the woman's figure beneath. And from that shadow, I could tell she was wearing little to nothing beneath the sheer robe. She was also stunningly beautiful with perfect waves of shimmering brown hair, bronze skin, and large amber eyes.

"You must be the newbies?" The woman said sitting down beside Silence and sliding an arm around him. He went rigid with fluster-shock. "I'm Lady Amber, captain of the second squad. She began teasing a slender-fingered hand up into Silence's brown hair. "I'm going to get one of you on my team. Ant will get the other on his." She had been addressing me, teasing Silence without so much as a glance, but she looked at him then. "I think I'll ask for this one." She took her hand from his hair, sliding it around his neck to under his chin, forcing his face to look up at hers. "What's your name, boy?"

He couldn't speak, staring directly into her amber eyes...

nowhere else... very focused. Her robe had fallen open just a little as she'd leaned toward him, and I was sure he'd get an eye-full if he looked down.

"Silence," I said for him. "His name is Silence." I didn't know how I felt about this. Mostly I felt sorry for my friend who didn't have a lot of experience with women and was being horribly teased.

A grin spread upon Amber's full, dark-red lips, then she laughed. "How very apt." She leaned closer, bringing her face alongside his, to nibble on his ear, then whispered. "A... *pleasure*... to meet you, Silence." Then she turned to me. "And you?"

"I'm... Legs."

She blinked at that. "And here I thought I'd always have the best legs in this strange family of ours. Well then, come on, stand up, let's get a look at them."

Now I was the one on the spot.

Lady Amber had said she was a squad captain, which meant she was definitely my superior — everyone here was my senior but she seemed to hold some additional authority — so I stood and moved to the side of the table, standing there awkwardly.

"Now, hike up that skirt and let me see these legs," Amber said. With this, she removed her hands from Silence who — once her attentions were on me — slumped in relief and slid away from her on the bench.

I'm fairly certain I turned beet red, feeling heat rise to my face... and every other part of me. "I... I..." I stammered incoherently for a long moment. It was my turn to be horribly teased, apparently. Amber was an equal opportunity teaser, it seemed.

"Here, I'll show you mine, if you like." She shifted off the bench and stood across from me. She pulled up her robe slowly, to mid-thigh, revealing a perfect leg. "Now your turn."

I figured I could do the same. It wouldn't be showing any more than the green dress I'd worn for my Nobles' Test. So, I pulled up my dress a little.

"Well damn, girl! Those are some bloody fine legs; long and lean. I think you've got me beat. It's that extra few inches of height you've got on me, all leg I bet." She didn't actually seem upset, more... playful.

"Stop bothering the new recruits!" The voice made me jump. It hadn't been loud, but it seemed to boom through the hall with resonant authority. I dropped the hem of my dress and spun, and there was Ant — appearing from nowhere once again — not far behind me. "Amber, you're insufferable some days!" He seemed more scolding than truly angry.

"You didn't think I was insufferable last night," Amber purred seductively. "I believe you whispered something about me being a 'sex goddess'?"

Ant blushed.

Oh... so she could get under *anybody's* skin; very interesting indeed.

I turned back to Amber, who was laughing lightly as she twirled around and headed for a screened passage at the end of the hall. "I'll grab something from the kitchens and leave the newbies be." Then she was gone, and the sexual tension in the room dropped from stifling to nothing.

I took a long breath.

"Excuse her," Ant said, coming to sit on a bench at a table across from where Silence and I had been. I sat again. Lord Ant was fully dressed, though the shirt didn't seem to do much to hide his massive frame and bulging muscles. He smiled kindly. "She's a tease, and... some... people like that."

He cleared his throat and nodded. "And I'd say she's harmless, but she's not. You don't get to be squad captain by being harmless."

"Amber?" I said slowly. It was an interesting name, giving little clue to her avatar. "What's her avatar?"

"A butterfly," Ant said with a grin. "Specifically, an Amber-Phantom butterfly."

Amber-Phantom? That sounded beautiful and mysterious... yup, that worked.

And while we were asking questions: "How do you keep popping up out of nowhere?" I asked Ant directly.

He laughed. "Think about it for a moment and you'll get there."

Think about what?

What's his name, Legs? Auwei hinted.

Ant?

And that's when it hit me. He wasn't appearing out of nowhere, he was being an ant, tiny and virtually unseen, then veering back into his human form.

"Oh!"

"Yeah, I knew you were smart." He nodded. "That's why I've asked for you on my squad."

"Me?" My mind whirled. "Meaning Silence will be on Amber's?"

Ant nodded slowly. "Yeah. I'll have a talk with Fennec, see if he can't help the boy while keeping Amber from teasing him too much."

"Fennec?" I asked. I couldn't figure out from the name what the man's avatar might be.

"You'll meet everyone in time. Just stay in the hall and they'll all wander in eventually. As much as Crane makes sure her breakfast is served promptly at seven, the cooks make sure there's something around all morning. The rest of us work on our own schedules most of the time while we're here. If we're on a mission, things are different. Then you do as you're told, when you're told, no questions, no hesitations, got it?"

I nodded. "Yes, Lord Ant."

He cringed. "Ant is fine. I don't need the title. I was a farm boy before all this and became a Noble to help out and defend the nation. I'm no lord."

I understood that sentiment. "It does feel funny," I said with a grimace. "Lady Legs just doesn't sound right."

"Ha! Yeah, I see. Well, then just Legs it is. I haven't had a chance to talk to Crane yet. What's your avatar?"

"A spider."

Some manner of jumping spider I'd guess, Auwei said. I didn't feel the need to relay that to Ant.

He nodded with a smile. "Nice! I'll have to keep a wary eye out."

"Why?" He was three times my size and could easily—

"Spiders eat ants," Silence mumbled.

"Oh... right..." I shook my head. "I'm still getting used to this whole avatar thing. It's a bit disorienting."

He nodded. "I get it. Imagine me becoming accustomed to being an ant."

True.

"And you, what's your avatar?" Ant asked Silence. "With a name like Silence it could be any number of things."

"A mouse."

He nodded. "Ah, yes, that makes sense." Then he laughed, a full-throated and hearty thing. "Well then, since you'll be on Amber's squad, just remember... Mice eat butterflies."

I blinked, looking over at Silence, who was a bit wide-eyed with surprise as well.

"And Cranes eat all of the above!" This sharp-tongued voice came from above us. I looked up to see a gallery balcony along three sides of the great hall. Lady Crane leaned upon the railing glaring down at us. I didn't know what she was doing, and she didn't deign to explain before she turned and left.

Ant chuckled. "True... so watch out for her."

"Are there any in Maverick House that aren't tiny creatures?" I asked.

Ant smiled and gave a knowing wink. "Oh... yes. You just wait and see."

As the morning wore on, we met the other members of the House, all but two. We kept hearing about Lady Midnight and her secret mission, but nothing more. The other missing member was Fin... whose avatar was a whale. He was out patrolling the ocean waters for pirates. But the rest we met that day.

Jack arrived for breakfast still completely naked, winking at me once again before heading into the kitchens.

"Ignore him," Ant said. "He's on my squad, and he likes to flirt and will probably make some advances on you, but if you tell him no, he'll listen."

That was good to know.

"That goes for you too," Ant said to Silence. "Jack... goes for all sorts."

Silence and I raised our brows at that, but same-sex pairings weren't uncommon in Elista. Silence nodded at the advice.

"Why is he..." I began.

"Naked?" Ant shrugged. "Just his thing. He only does it while he's here, out on missions he's fully dressed and a deadly fighter, quick and lethal."

Also good to know.

The next to arrive were two men who looked similar enough to each other I guessed they were brothers. What had Lady Crane called them? Fennec and Foggy? They came over and made introductions. Neither were large men, Fennec was only a bit taller than me, short for a man, and very lean; wiry was a good word to describe him. He had pale brown hair, almost dirty-blond and friendly hazel eyes. He had a way of twitching his head as if he was constantly hearing something distracting.

"A Fennec is a type of fox, very small, with large ears," he said, describing his avatar. He then went to talk to Silence after Ant told him to take the young man under his wing.

Foggy, on the other hand, was... just plain odd. He was even shorter than his brother, one of the few full-grown men I looked down at, yet he was a bit more filled out, though still lean of frame.

"Fog beetle," he said shaking my hand. Then... for no particular reason, released me and did a lithe half-flip, landing lightly on his arms and settling into a very relaxed hand-stand. "Nice to meet you." He had darker hair than his brother but the same hazel eyes. And he too moved his head in odd ways, but more extreme, tilting and moving around to seemingly look at everything from every angle all at once.

"He's on my squad," Ant said. "And you'll... get used to him in time. He may not be normal, but he has some very interesting ways of seeing things and perspectives on situations like no one else."

As the brothers were leaving, another pair entered, both women, and as different as two people could be. One was very large, heavy-set, and a head taller than me, which made her a unique woman indeed. The second was small, quite slight of build, and a bit fidgety.

"Tusk," the larger woman introduced herself. "A boar."

"She's the muscle on Amber's squad," Ant said.

The tall woman had wiry, unkempt dark-brown hair with a dark complexion, bright and clear yellow eyes, and a wide smile.

"It is a pleasure to meet you, Legs. I'm Sparrow," said the other woman. That name immediately made sense. She was small and a bit erratic of movement, like her namesake, with large green eyes and a small mouth. Her hair was a light red-brown. I liked her instantly, and she seemed to sense that, smiling at me.

"A scout, also on Amber's squad," Ant said.

"We're going to get some food and head to the library, would you like to join us?" Sparrow asked.

"I'd love that, thank you!" I said instantly. "I might stick around here until I've met the rest of the household, but I'll meet you there if I'm not needed elsewhere." This with a look at Ant.

"The first day is all yours. Your training begins tomorrow, bright and earlyish at eight. Be out in the back courtyard and ready to work." With that, he rose. "Feel free to stick around here or go with Tusk and Sparrow, but the last member of the House may not be down for a while. Princess... likes to sleep *a lot*."

"There is often a sun-spot in the library where she curls up around this time of day, if you come with us, we can introduce you," Sparrow said.

So, after they'd gone to the kitchens for some food, Silence and I followed Tusk and Sparrow to the library.

And there, curled up in a sunspot, as promised, was a plump, ginger-coated cat.

"Princess!" Sparrow said going to her, then flinching back as Princess twitched awake. Right... birds would be afraid of cats. "We have a new member. This is Legs. She's a spider."

Princess rolled onto her back, presenting her belly to me. Odd as it was to think of this as my Housemate, I did as — I hoped — she intended, and went over to rub her belly. She purred.

When I sat back, she veered into her human form, sitting before me with a drowsy smile. "Nice to meet you, Legs."

"And this is Silence," Sparrow said. "A mouse."

Instantly Princess' attention snapped to Silence, eyes going wide. "*Very* nice to meet you!" she practically purred the words.

Silence flinched back.

Princess... was odd indeed. Very feline in her demeanor. She had bouncy pale ginger curls, with intent orange eyes. I couldn't rightly tell, since we were both sitting, but she did not seem tall, and was definitely a bit on the rounder side, reminding me of Blackclaw. She was certainly full-figured through bust and hips, but dressed in loose flowing clothes so it was hard to tell her exact form.

"Now, if you'll excuse me..." and she was back as a cat again, purring, curling back up in her sunspot.

"She stays like that, in her avatar form, most of the time while here at Hedgewild," Tusk said, shaking her head.

She was a cat; why wouldn't she?

I couldn't help but stroke her fine ginger fur, and she purred louder.

And that was that. I'd met all of the members of House Maverick, except the ones that weren't here.

It was an eclectic lot, but I sensed a bond between them. A bond I hoped Silence and I would merge with eventually.

Right now, I still felt like an outsider. But that day Sparrow took the time to make Silence and I feel welcome. We chatted with her in the library for some time, learning all the ins and outs of this strange family, and the estate. By the end of the day, Silence and I were laughing easily with the witty young woman, instant friends. Sparrow even gave Silence the scoop on Amber and how to handle her, since they would be on the same squad together. The young man seemed far more at ease.

And just like that... this place began to feel like home.

The next day our training started... and the pain began.

CHAPTER 18

"Not bad!" Ant said nodding his approval. Meanwhile, I was shaking my aching, tingling fist, knuckles sore. I kept stretching my hand to stop the throbbing. Punching Ant was not something I wanted to do again. He was hard as rock!

That was how he'd started our martial training: "Punch me," he'd said. "Trust me I'll be well enough."

And I believed him now.

He was shirtless again and... just wow. All that rounded muscle looked a bit cushiony, but it wasn't. It was solid.

"Ants have a shell, remember," he said by way of explanation. "It takes a lot to hurt me."

Good to know.

"Your turn," Ant said turning to Silence, who blanched and shook his head.

Ant laughed. "A shy one, are we? Don't worry, we'll train that out of you. Nobles need to be able to face many different situations and protect the nation when called upon. Here, we mostly fight pirates, and that's not often. But still, you need to be ready. So go ahead, hit me as hard as you can."

Silence looked at me. I nodded for him to try. He shrugged, balled his fist, thumb tucked inside, and swung.

"Silen—" I tried to stop him. With how he'd made his fist, he'd break his thumb. But I didn't get there in time. He hit Ant.

Crack went his thumb and Silence shrieked in pain, retrieving his hand back to hold protectively, tears coming to his eyes.

Ant waved me off, kneeling before Silence. "Let me see," he said tenderly. It took a couple of tries before Silence let the large man look at his hand.

Ant took the hand and surrounded it with both of his — much larger — hands. Then he closed his eyes, took a deep breath, and seemed to concentrate. I watched, fascinated. So did Silence who sniffed back his tears as a look of blinking wonder came over him.

"There, better?" Ant said, releasing the hand.

Silence nodded. He wiggled his fingers and thumb, then smiled. "You can heal?"

Ant nodded. "I can heal."

"Is that an ant thing?" I asked, a bit stupefied.

"No," Ant said softly. "Has anyone ever told you about spirit-gifts?"

We shook our heads.

Ant sat, and even sitting was still taller than Silence, but not me. "Some True-Bonded, who have been with their Lumani for a while, and are strong in spirit, develop special abilities."

Oh... that sounded familiar.

I told you about them, not that long ago, at Silverveil. Though I didn't recall the name for them at the time. None of my Hosts has ever possessed such abilities. Ant must be a powerful True-Bonded if he has them.

I listened intently as he went on. "Several of us in Maverick's crew have them." He chuckled. "If you think I can sneak up on you, wait till you meet Midnight. She can be as silent as the space between thoughts, and be standing right next to you, and you'd never know."

She sounded powerful and mysterious. I sort of loved that everyone talked about her with such awe. It made me want to meet her all the more, and also... terrified of her.

"And Fin, our resident whale, he's developed the ability to instantly move between locations, but he can only go to a place he knows. I can heal, and Amber... she can take control of a person's mind."

"Control of their mind?" I blurted. "That's..."

"Yeah, she doesn't do it often, and doesn't like to do it." He hesitated. "Well, I don't know how much she likes to do it. She says she doesn't like it, but... these powers you see, they come from... something deeper within us, a fundamental part of our spirit manifesting itself. I heal because I have a drive to help people, do things for them, aid them. Fin loves to travel and see different places. Midnight loves to be hidden and secretive. Amber... my theory is... she loves to be noticed, the entire focus of a person's attention, so... mind control."

He smiled at both of us. "I wouldn't be surprised if you develop a spirit-gift someday. Maverick has a knack for picking people with strong spirits. Not everyone in the House has one, just us four and Maverick... so far. They often take some time to develop. I was in my early twenties before I began to sense... something, and it took years to harness it and use it effectively."

Fascinating.

Isn't it, though? Auwei was just a bit haughty sounding

when she added, *I think of all my Hosts, you have the greatest potential to have such gifts.*

You think so?

I do. You're special, Legs. I know it.

Wow, thanks. I wish I felt that way.

That's part of what makes you special. You're modest about it. But that's also keeping your potential restrained, I think. Whenever you have your bold moments, like wearing that dress the first day at Silverveil, or your Nobles' Test, that's when I feel it. There is more to you. You'll see.

I smiled, sending Auwei a sense of gratitude.

Since Ant had mentioned it and not gone into detail, I had to ask, "What's Maverick's gift?"

Ant smiled. "He doesn't like me sharing. You'll have to ask him yourself someday."

Yeah, that wasn't going to happen any time soon. The well-built leader of our House still intimidated The Pits out of me. He also hadn't returned from the capital yet.

"Now!" Ant said rising. "Back to training. After those punches, I have a sense for your skill and natural ability. I'll work out a training program for each of you. Today, we'll just work on basics." He paused then, looking at me curiously. "Is it true you killed three assassins at Silverveil?"

Yup, that's me. "And nearly died in the process."

"Still..."

"Also, one of them was pure luck," I added. "A trap I'd set worked very well."

"But that means two weren't luck." He nodded. "I think you'll be moving on to the advanced course soon enough." He looked at both of us. "Until then, you're all mine. Pick up those practice swords, and we'll run through some forms."

The rest of the morning was spent learning three basic sword forms. We ended with some simple sparring, myself and Ant that was, Silence wasn't ready for that yet. I held my forms well enough, though I did get a solid slap on my hip with a practice sword when I over-extended on a shoulder strike. Ant didn't heal that minor injury. He said it would remind me not to make the same mistake again. By the end of the first week... I had a lot of reminders.

Mornings were martial training; afternoons were studies in a variety of other topics. I was already well educated so I moved on to more advanced subjects like state-craft and strategy, well before Silence did. The two of us also attended classes on how to develop our avatar abilities, which... was a slow process for me. Auwei was certain there was more I could accomplish, but nothing became apparent. I did get better, and more controlled at the few things I could do, though. And I was finally able to take my avatar form. I spent a day off exploring the house as a spider and found it terrifying. Everything was so much larger than I was... even a few other spiders.

Soon enough I graduated the basic combat class, no longer training with Silence. He was slow to pick up combat training. While I — as Ant had predicted — quickly moved on to the advanced classes. They were with Jack, and he was a completely different man during training, all business with quick and deadly precision. He also didn't take it easy on me, but that made me learn all the quicker and by the end of my first month at Hedgewild, I was sporting fewer bruises and feeling like I might actually be a productive Noble one day.

Silence and I saw less and less of each other, but still managed to grab a few moments together, sometimes alone, sometimes with Sparrow. But more and more, Silence was dedicating himself to study. He had a lot to learn and spent extra hours poring over books or practicing combat forms.

Which meant much of my spare time was spent with Sparrow. I was surprised to learn she was three years older than me. She seemed so small and free-spirited: youthful.

A month passed. Maverick hadn't returned from the capital and Midnight was still on her "secret" mission. But I was getting to know all the other members of Maverick House.

Jack ended one of our practice sessions with an offer to join him in the baths. I declined, and he didn't bring it up again. Amber didn't tease me... as much, and Ant was beginning to feel like a protective older brother, if a really handsome one. I still had no clue how to deal with Foggy, but then... neither did his brother, Fennec; no one did.

I got to know the feel of the place. How Tusk and Ant were usually up early and helping the farmers or gardeners around the estate. Where Princess would have her naps and that she did indeed spend virtually all of her time as a cat, except when eating or occasionally socializing. It became common to find Foggy in random parts of the house, doing head-stands or poking into dark corners. Fin came to visit a few times, a large man, even taller than Ant, but where Ant was all muscle, Fin was... not. He was brawny and sturdy and heavy, but still moved nimbly enough.

I got to know Amber's moods. She could be testy and stand-offish some days, but friendly and effervescent on others. No one talked about it, so it took me a while to figure out that she was always cheerier on days after she'd seduced Ant the night before. Fraternizing between Housemates wasn't forbidden, but I came to understand that it was generally frowned upon, mostly by Lady Crane. But since Amber could be a bit wild some days, Ant would "take one for the team" to keep her in high spirits. I don't think he minded, but part of him was still an innocent farm boy and, Spirits, how he could blush when it was mentioned.

Time passed, my twenty-first birthday came and went; there was a party. Despite my promises to my sister, I drank too much and woke up with another heady hangover. Silence had his eighteenth birthday; we'd both been born in the fall, apparently. That night, I offered to stay with him, but he declined. He looked exhausted all the time now, and yet, I'd never seen him happier. He laughed with Sparrow and me, even others from time to time, and seemed to love learning new things. I was happy for him, though I felt like we were drifting apart. I told myself he needed time to make up for all the learning he'd missed as a child. I hoped that was true.

I was also learning a lot, much more confident in my skills and martial prowess. I was anxious to prove myself.

Then, finally, came my first mission.

CHAPTER 19

Fin appeared in the great hall, interrupting the evening meal. Since he'd transported himself directly here from the ocean, he was dripping wet, long pale-brown hair plastered to his round head. His slightly bulbous grey eyes blinked as they searched and found us. "Pirates," the heavy-set man said. "We need to go now, before we lose them."

Amber wasn't present, so Ant took control. With a quick look around, he nodded. "My squad, grab your gear, we head out as soon as you can make it back here." But his full squad wasn't there, Princess was off sleeping, most likely. But Fennec and Sparrow were there and he quickly turned to them. "You two are with us. Fennec, prep for a fight. Sparrow, you'll be on watch." She nodded, and a hardness that I hadn't seen before came over the small woman's eyes.

Jack, luckily, had just ended a session of small-scale combat theory with me, so he was fully dressed and had his weapons on him.

I turned to him. "Do I have weapons?" With a movement faster than I could see he'd tossed a dagger and it was sticking out of the table in front of me.

"Use that, stay out of the way, watch and learn. Stay in your avatar form once we're on the ship, no one will notice you. We don't expect you to fight your first time out." He stood and checked himself over quickly, slipping back on the heavy leather jerkin he'd taken off earlier. "You're good, Legs, and you've learned a lot quickly, but it's different being in the thick of a fight."

I nodded.

The others were soon ready.

Ant turned to me. "You ready for this? You don't have to come."

"I'm ready," I said, hoping I didn't sound terrified. In truth, I had no clue how I'd be in the thick of a real life-and-death fight. When I'd been attacked by those assassins, I'd reacted on instinct, then I'd Bonded and Auwei had helped a lot. This was different. I knew I was headed for something dangerous and I had time to think about it. Somehow that made it worse, all possible — mostly bad — scenarios playing through my mind.

I'll protect you, Auwei said and I knew she would. Though, even as I linked hands with the others, I recalled what Auwei had done, when she'd taken control of me during the fight with the assassins in the baths. I felt like I could do those things now, after months of training. I actually did feel... ready.

Then the world spun and I gasped as cold water splashed and surged around me. I slid under the waves, then came up sputtering.

The others were more prepared. They'd done this before. Fin went from being a large man to... a massive whale. That pushed us out from him a little. Ant caught me and pulled me up as everyone clambered on top of the huge form. Sparrow was up and away as a bird. Foggy veered into a beetle, wings out, also flying toward the ship...

The ship was close, moving toward us. It seemed Fin had anticipated where the ship would be and had returned us to a spot roughly in its path. Now it was barreling down on us. The rest of us held on tight as Fin submerged a little, keeping us above water, to move us into position.

It was evening, the sun just above the horizon in the west. Enough light to see by, but soon there wouldn't be.

"Left side," Ant said, leaning down over Fin, tapping the whale beneath him. I didn't think whales could hear, so the words had been for us. I guessed that the tapping of the large form beneath us had been indicating which way to go.

Fin shifted slightly and swam us toward the indicated side of the ship. Or more precisely, we didn't move much but Fin got us in a position so when the ship passed by, we'd be close enough to climb aboard.

Ant whispered to us. "We'll be coming up with the sun behind us. We'll be silhouetted and easy to see, but they'll have the sun in their eyes at least for a moment or two before it sets. Let's use that to our advantage." He looked around. "We're more than a match for a pirate crew, nasty and vicious as they may be. Keep together and stay sharp." He turned to Jack. "Carry me." Then he veered and was almost washed away as an ant, before Jack scooped him up and placed the small insect on his shoulder.

"The rest of us are good jumpers," Jack said, voice low, the ship close. "But ants can't jump."

I nodded.

Fin sank a little deeper, hiding us as much as possible. When the ship drew alongside us, Fin swept us closer and the remaining three of us jumped as one. I jumped the highest, intentionally this time, and landed on the spar holding up the mainsail. Then I instantly shifted into a spider to watch the fight below.

The crew was more than a little shocked when two men jumped up on deck and even more surprised when two more men — Ant and Foggy — appeared in their midst a moment later. The pirates, at a quick count, looked to number perhaps close to twenty, though I quickly amended that count as more ran up on deck. There were thirty at least.

Thirty on four? Ant had seemed confident before, but I was suddenly worried for my companions below.

Then they began to fight. Jack used a slender-bladed rapier in one hand and a long parrying dagger in the other. Ant used a thick quarterstaff, spinning it in defense, while tripping up his foes and bashing them into oblivion. Fennec had knives, lots of knives; he'd throw one and another would appear in his hand. Foggy didn't so much fight as confound his foes, dancing and capering around the ship, narrowly avoiding so many lethal blows, while somehow managing to nudge, kick, or trip foes such that they often died on the weapons of their allies. Very quickly it was four on twenty; then four on fifteen and...

There came a sharp, high, trembling cry from nearby; a sparrow's call. I looked around quickly and saw what Sparrow was indicating. A woman, dressed in fine and flowing robes was standing on the stairs to the lower decks, watching the fight as I was. Then... she looked up at me and smiled.

How in The Pits did she know I was there?

I have a bad feeling about her, Auwei muttered. I had to agree.

With a wave of the woman's hand a fine spray of mist shot out from her fingers and shot across the deck, by the time it reached where the fighting was, it was a wall of mist which slammed into everyone — pirates and Nobles alike — knocking them off their feet, throwing them across the wooden boards.

A mistweaver! Auwei's terror flowed through me

Bloody Bones! I would have cursed out lout, if I could have.

The woman strode slowly, purposefully up onto the deck. She looked up at me again. "Time to come down, little spider." And with a grasping motion a ball of mist appeared around me and held me tight, pulling me from the yard, to float down to the deck.

Hazra! I knew it was her, even though I'd never seen her before. *But how?*

She knew...

A cold feeling filled me, settling first in my gut and spreading icy fingers into my very muscles and bones. Yes, she'd known where I was, that Maverick House fought the coastal pirates off the south of Elista. She'd known and set a trap for me.

But why me? I still couldn't answer that.

"I want to see your face when I kill you, slippery one," she said, and the fog surrounding me seemed to seep within me. I tried to hold my avatar form, even if only to confound her, but the mists ate at my very nature, eroded it until I was forced back into my human body. I sat on the deck, near the side of the ship, as she approached. The tiny ball of fog that had surrounded me as a spider was gone, so I tried to rise,

"No," she commanded with a grin and I was stopped, mists appeared over my feet and around my waist, neck, and wrists, keeping me in place.

"Why?" I called out to her, even as the mist — like iron

bands — around my neck began to constrict and cut off my air.

She strode over to stand before me, slightly shorter, but seeming so very large and powerful, radiating an aura of intensity I couldn't ignore. I was terrified and so was Auwei.

With a subtle wave of her hands, fog surrounded her feet and lifted her so she looked down upon me. Her eyes burned with madness. "Why?" she whispered with a manic grin. "Because I like to kill," she said with a tilt of her head. "And you're in the way of our plans. Well, not yet, but you will be, and we can't have that, now can we?"

I flicked my gaze to where the men lay. Ant was rising, the others starting to regain themselves.

"They can't help you, child," the mistweaver said and with another casual wave of her hand, sent them all flying. "I made a mistake last time, hiring out your death. This time I'll do it myself and, just for fun, I'll make it slow and painful. Would you like that? No, probably not, but *I'll* like it."

She's insane, Auwei gasped in horror.

Yeah, I was getting that.

She stepped back as the bonds around the various parts of me began to tighten. I'd already been struggling to breathe, but now I was completely without air. My waist, wrists, and feet were being constricted and crushed as well. I would have screamed if I could. Then — because this wasn't bad enough — Hazra made a sort of sprinkling motion with her hand and pain, like a hundred needle-points pressed into me from every angle.

The pain was unlike anything I'd ever felt before, true agony. Tears leaked from my eyes, which bulged with my desperate need to breathe.

The mistweaver laughed. "I want to hear one scream

before you die," she said, and the restraint on my neck eased just enough for a gulp of air. Then — as much as I didn't want to comply with her desires — I screamed in anguish. One long, clear cry, then the neck-binding tightened again, this time working faster, crushing my neck.

The world shrunk. Darkness threatened the edges of my vision and despite my desperation to live, I also craved that darkness and an end to this pain. All I could see was her, that pale face, blissful as she watched me die.

Then... a small white and brown shape attacked the woman's face. Sparrow.

Hazra screamed, waving her hands.

My bonds released, but I was too weak and too broken to do anything but crumple into a heap. I couldn't breathe, my throat still crushed. And with the next roll of the ship, I slid off the deck entirely.

The ocean swallowed me in cold oblivion, water pouring into my mouth. I couldn't stop it. I couldn't do anything. Darkness closed in again as I sank deeper and deeper.

Then... nothing.

CHAPTER 20

ACCORDING TO THE OTHERS, I DIDN'T ACTUALLY DIE.

But it sure felt like it.

Air flowed into my lungs, and I gasped and sputtered out seawater. I was rolled onto my side as light stabbed into my eyes and waves of tremendous pain surged through my entire being. I had no energy to cry out, so I just whimpered.

"Amber!" I heard a voice shout.

Everything was hazy, my eyesight dim, but I saw a fall of auburn hair and intense amber eyes. "Sleep," came the soft but intense word and I had to obey it. I fell into unconsciousness again.

When next I woke from the black depths of a dreamless sleep, I blinked my eyes open to dim light, and a tremendous amount of pain. My hips ached and my feet throbbed. There still seemed to be a thousand points of fire across my skin, but they were fading, less urgent, more like a burning itch now. Though, my hands and throat were no longer sore. Curious.

Still, I groaned.

Sparrow came into view. "Legs?"

I groaned again. "Water?" I tried to say, but my voice was rough and raw. Sparrow seemed to understand and had a glass to my lips a moment later, lifting my head to help me drink. The water wasn't cold, but it felt so very soothing on its way down. While my head was lifted, I saw Ant, sitting slumped against the wall. He barely seemed to be breathing. I groaned again as Sparrow lifted the glass away, nodding my head toward him.

She looked, then looked back at me. "He's just resting. Your wounds are too severe. He can't heal them all at once, and it takes a lot out of him when he does.

Ah, that would be why my throat and hands weren't in pain anymore.

"You should rest, if you can," Sparrow urged, laying me back down.

I didn't see much point in remaining awake, so I slipped back into sleep once more. And that was how the next few days went. I woke, the pain present but diminished, and took some water or a bit of food. Silence or Sparrow was always there to spoon-feed me if needed. Ant was always there and always exhausted.

Then, finally, I woke feeling rested and refreshed, no pain at all. The room was dark, a single flickering lantern showing Sparrow curled up on a mattress on the floor. Ant was gone.

There was a noise, low and distant and it took me a moment to realize it was people talking somewhere close, but outside my room. I strained to hear what they were saying.

Don't listen with your ears, Auwei said. *You have another sense.*

Right! My spider's sense. I concentrated, feeling all my

hairs prick up, gooseflesh covering me... then the voices became clearer.

"...attack her here?" someone said, it sounded like Crane.

"If they were going to, they would have, long before now. They had months before that pirate ship. No, they know she's well-guarded here." This was a firm baritone voice, one I hadn't heard in a while... Maverick? Was he here?

"She's a mistweaver for Spirits' sake!" This from Amber, I knew that voice well enough. "The lot of us are no match for a mistweaver. She could waltz in here and slay all of us with ease. No, there's another reason she hasn't attacked us here." She sounded afraid. I'd never heard her so frightened before.

Maverick grunted.

"Amber's right." This from Ant, another voice I knew well. "I saw her power, none of you did. She could have easily killed all of us, but went only for Legs. I think..." Ant trailed off.

"What?" Maverick asked, gruff. "I trust your instincts Ant. Say it."

"I think she doesn't want to or... or can't kill the rest of us? She only wants to kill Legs, a tactical strike."

"Oh! Yes, of course!" This from Crane. "I think I might know why, but perhaps here is not the best place for us to talk. Come with me." And I heard footfalls fading down the hall.

I wanted to hear what Crane had to say. I was feeling well enough to get out of bed, so I slipped from under the covers. I wore only a light shift. That would have to do since I didn't want to waste time dressing. I slipped, silent as a spider, across to the door, not waking Sparrow.

The door creaked something fierce when I opened it, but Sparrow must have been out cold as she didn't even flinch.

The others were just turning into the long cross hallway at the center of the estate as I peered out into the hall.

I hurried to catch up, stopping at the corner to spy around and see them step into the central stairwell. There was only one place they could be going: the dome at the top of the central tower of Hedgewild.

Once they were all out of sight, I crept along to the stairwell. But... I'd heard this door creak a lot when opened previously, so I went a different way. I backed up to the entrance to the great hall, on the second floor this took me onto the balcony around the hall. From my explorations of Hedgewild, I knew that there was another access to the central stairs from here and no door, just an open archway to pass through. It was just to my left. So, I sneaked through that and slowly moved up the stairs. I got to the landing below the large domed room at the top of the tower and stopped there, keeping to the shadows. I could only just barely hear the whispers above, not able to make out the exact words, so I let my spider's sense do its thing once again.

My hair bristled, and the sounds came into focus.

"Out with it Crane, what's your theory?" This from Maverick.

Crane spoke, voice hushed. "Are we certain this room is warded? I've always wondered about that." She sounded uneasy, with a hint of awe in her voice.

"So Gander told me, when he passed leadership of the House to me. I've never had any reason to doubt the old man. Everything I've said in this room has stayed here. The only way anyone could hear is if they were actually here, not by any other means."

There was a long silence after that. My skin crawled. Did they know I was here, somehow, listening in?

I concentrated on hearing any movement with my enhanced senses and... there was something: a soft, almost imperceptible skittering of tiny feet. Curious about this, I focused, pin-pointing the sound. I heard two sets of tiny feet. One... a set of six skittering feet was *very* close.

Ant appeared right in front of me. "Hello, Legs. Glad to see you're up and about."

"I knew it! I knew someone was listening!" This from Amber up above.

"This concerns her, send her up," Maverick said, tone leaving no room for questions.

"You heard the boss," Ant said. "I'll stay down here and keep an eye out."

I nodded and went up the stairs to the top room. I'd only ever been in The Dome a few times. It was accessible to the House members, but it was held as a bit of a sacred space, so people went there sparingly. It was also Maverick's office, which made it awkward to stay for long periods. The tower itself was large, a twenty-five by twenty-five foot square. The stone walls continued up to around waist height as if this had once been an open turret. Perhaps the dome had been added later? The dome itself was clear glass, with a bit of a greenish tint. It began square at the base, following the line of the wall, then slowly morphed into the spherical covering.

Outside was dark, an overcast night. There were two large hearths in the room, on the east and west sides. In the middle of the room, close to one hearth, was a large desk and a couple free-standing book shelves. By the other hearth, was a large sitting area. The north side, where I was now, and the south side, were mostly open. In late fall, with no fires in either hearth, it was quite cool up here, especially for me in my nightdress.

As I looked around from the top of the stairs, I saw the source of the other set of tiny footprints I'd heard... a tiny grey and white mouse, keeping to the cracks in the stonework of the walls.

Hello Silence, I said internally and smiled. Apparently, he'd been listening in on all of this... probably from back at my room as well. He wanted to know what was going on as much as I did. I wouldn't expose him.

Crane fetched a heavy blanket, which had been folded over the back of a long couch in the seating area, then came to me, draping the warm cloth over me.

"You'll catch a chill, child," she said with motherly concern. Then she led me to the heavy rug which covered the floor under the sitting area, my feet on the cold stones had been uncomfortable indeed.

Maverick snapped his fingers and a fire leaped to life on the logs set in the hearth by the sitting area.

I started at that.

So *that* was his spirit-gift? I wondered what "fire" meant, what it was he "loved" to get that ability.

We all took seats.

Crane sat next to me, arm around me like a mother hen. She looked at me for a long time, lips pursed. "Do you know who wants to kill you? Or why?"

I *had* learned a bit. "I know the mistweaver's name is Hazra. She said..." I tried to recall more. My memory of the events on the ship were fuzzy, probably from my lack of air during the encounter. "She said... she liked to kill, but... it was more than that. She *needed* to kill me because I was... in the way?" No, that wasn't right.

She said, "You're in the way of our plans. Well, not yet, but you will be, and we can't have that, now can we?" You were a bit distracted, but I knew if we survived, we'd want to remember that.

Thank you, Auwei. I repeated the words for the others.

"You're not yet in the way, but you will be?" Amber muttered. "Then..."

"Yes, they have some means of seeing the future. Whoever *they* are," Maverick said, jaw set hard.

"That's where I have a theory," Crane said. She hugged me a little closer. "I think... other Nobles are behind this."

Amber started, eyes wide with disbelief. "No!" she gasped. "That's ridiculous. Nobles of Elista, trying to kill other Nobles? That's madness!"

I only nodded. I didn't understand yet, but I knew Crane would explain.

Oddly, Maverick didn't seem shocked at all.

He knows something. Perhaps that's why he remained in the capital for so long. Something's going on with the other Nobles.

"It makes sense," Maverick said, nodding. "It's why they don't want to kill the rest of us. Legs is in the way of their plans, whatever those plans may be, but to kill off an entire Noble House... that would bring attention they don't want. So, they need to kill one Noble very precisely and quietly without the rest of us being harmed... much." He shook his head. "Bloody-stinking-bones. Those bastards!"

"You sound like you know who it is?" I said, curious.

He shook his head. "No... I don't *know*. I *suspect*." He sighed heavily. "I think it's time I told you why I've been away so long." He took a long moment to collect his thoughts in silence.

I trembled with fear and anticipation.

Maverick ran a hand through his rough, spikey hair and heaved another sigh. "What I'm going to tell you doesn't leave this room. Understood?" He looked at me, hard, unyielding. "You're new. I wouldn't normally tell you this sort of thing, but it seems to involve you, so you're in. But that means you have to keep this secret as well. You tell no one. Not even the other members of our House, as it might unduly scare them. Definitely no one *outside* our House. We don't know who we can trust. Understood?"

We all nodded.

"I want to hear you say it," Maverick insisted.

"Understood," Lady Crane said seriously.

"Tell no one, got it," Amber said.

At this point, I knew I should divulge my little secret. "Ahhh..."

"What is it?" Maverick asked.

I called, raising my voice a little. "Silence, you should probably come out now."

"Silence?" Crane asked.

Shocked expressions appeared on all three of the other's faces. I turned to see the man standing in his usual sleeping attire: loose breeches and nothing else, standing near the wall by the stairwell.

I'd seen him off and on over the last half-year and he'd grown a lot in that time, not just physically, but in confidence. He was still quiet and reserved, but there was a surety to his stance now, a liveliness to his step. He'd also grown several inches and was roughly a match for me in height and build.

"Ah, hi," he said, blushing, looking like he'd been caught spying... which he had.

"Spirits, I didn't hear... that's amazing!" Maverick breathed. Then he looked at me. "How'd *you* know?"

"I have special super-hearing. I heard him when I was back on the stairs."

"He's literally quiet as a mouse, and you heard him?" Amber said, shocked. "His name is Bloody *Silence* for Spirit's sake!"

I shrugged.

"Sorry," Silence said, voice low. "I ah... I heard you talking about Legs in the halls downstairs and got curious."

Maverick sighed. "Well you know too much now, come and sit. But you and Legs need to swear you'll not tell anyone what I'm about to tell you."

Crane went and got a second blanket for Silence as he came to sit with me. We shared a smile then both turned to Maverick.

"I swear," Silence said.

"I won't tell a soul," I added. I was a little trepidatious about all of this. What was so important we couldn't even tell members of our own House?

Whatever it is, you can trust these people and you always have me. I'll take care of you, Auwei said.

That helped reassure me, a little.

Maverick drew a long breath. "Something's been happening to Nobles. Over the last two years or so, Nobles have been dying, some under mysterious circumstances, some not." He paused there, looking at each of us in turn. "That in itself isn't that odd, people die all the time. But some of these deaths have been *very* concerning. It's not something that's widely known — only the leaders of the Houses have been told the full details — but it seems that for some of these deaths... the Lumani within the Noble died as well."

Auwei gasped. I felt her shock, confusion, and horror.

Crane and Amber let out similar noises.

Silence looked confused, but I understood. Lumani were immortal, and shouldn't be able to die. Slowly, a look of understanding and horror came to Silence's face as Haleia must have informed him.

Exactly, Auwei said. *We are energy and when our host passes, we live on as energy. We're saddened by the loss, but we live. It shouldn't be possible for a Lumani to die with their host. Unless...*

"A mistweaver?" I said slowly, finishing Auwei's thought. I recalled that Auwei had said something about mistweavers being able to kill Lumani after the attack at Silverveil.

"Yes," Maverick answered. "Some of the leaders think it's possible a mistweaver has found a way to kill host and Lumani as one. Though others still think Mistweavers are legends and there has to be another explanation. Honestly, I was in that group... until I heard what happened on the pirate ship."

He blew out a long breath. "According to you, the mist-weaver used the words 'we' and 'our.' And before I knew a mistweaver existed, I was beginning to suspect certain Nobles of these heinous deeds. I still suspect them."

He ground his teeth, jaw tense. I could tell he was struggling with this next bit. He didn't know if he should tell us or not. With another sigh, and a shake of his head I knew he'd decided to say it. "I think... it could even go as high as the queen herself."

"Spirits, no!" Lady Crane gasped.

I was too shocked to speak. I couldn't believe it either.

It was Amber, who was the most composed of all of us. "Why do you think that?" she asked softly.

He shook his head. "I don't know for certain, but... I can't imagine this sort of thing getting very far without someone pretty high up being in on it. Trouble is, if the queen or any of the other House Leaders are involved, I couldn't discern that when I was in the capital. I was there for months and saw no signs of deceit." He looked into the fire, frustration written on his rugged features. "And neither did Midnight."

"Midnight?" I asked. The mysterious member of our House, off on some secret mission. "Her mission was to spy on the other Nobles?" I guessed.

Maverick nodded. "But she's found nothing so far. The trouble is... there are a lot of Nobles, and she can't spy on all of them at once. So far, whoever is behind all of this is being *very* careful. I've kept her in the capital for now, hoping she'll find something, but..." He shrugged and didn't go on.

This is horrible, Auwei hissed, clearly still reeling from the news of the dead Lumani.

Ah, yeah. Our lives are in danger, both of us, so yeah, I'd say that's pretty horrible!

"So, just to get this straight," I said, voice trembling. "A mistweaver is trying to kill me, but not hurt the rest of you because that would alert too many people. That makes us think Nobles are behind this. And some Nobles are killing off other Nobles, maybe using a mistweaver... oh, and they can see the future. That's great..." Recapping things hadn't made me feel any better.

"Why? Why do any of this?" I asked.

Maverick shook his head. "I don't know," he growled softly. "There's something big going on here, but I have no clue what it is. I'm sorry, Legs."

"They must have some larger plan," Amber said. "Something that's potentially already in motion. And... and those they killed either were getting in the way or would get in the way in the future... like Legs."

Maverick nodded. "Sounds about right. Just wish I knew what it was."

This is wrong, Auwei said firmly. *If... if Nobles are behind this, that means their Lumani are complicit in the killing of other Lumani. That's unheard of. That's—*

Horrible? Yeah, I'm beginning to understand the full depths of the horribleness of all this.

Spirits! Auwei cursed.

Exactly.

CHAPTER 21

I BECAME A SHUT-IN. MORE THAN THAT, I WAS LIMITING WHAT our House could do, since one squad had to remain near me at all times. My training moved inside; they wouldn't even let me out into the gardens.

I'm afraid to say, I got a little morose and bitter, lashing out at people when I didn't mean it. Sparrow stayed by me, even though I didn't always treat her kindly. For that, I'll always love her. Silence saw me when he could, but he was still very busy with his work. I wanted his company more than ever, but I didn't ask for it. I was concerned that if this mistweaver found out about the two of us she'd use my feelings for him against us, perhaps capture him or... worse. So I stayed away from him as my heart broke just a little more.

When Ant's squad was away, taking both Ant and Jack, I'd train with Amber. I didn't think she'd have much to teach me.

I was wrong.

I landed hard on my back, my head bouncing off the special mats stuffed with straw. They were a bit of padding between my aching body and the hard floor, but didn't cushion that much. I groaned.

"What was that?" I asked, remaining flat on my back.

Amber hadn't even been using a weapon. I'd lunged at her with my practice sword, only to find myself laid out. We were in a long room in the east wing, which was specially designed for indoor combat practice. It was bare save for the mats on the floor and a few racks of weapons.

Nothing I have seen before, Auwei said, tone holding just a bit of awe. *I've heard of men from distant lands who fight open handed and can manipulate the energies within their own bodies, as well as the bodies of others, but... never seen it before, if that's what this is.*

Amber sighed. "As I thought. Those idiot men have been teaching you all wrong."

"Wrong?" I thought I'd been doing well. I was faster than Ant now and could even land a hit on Jack occasionally.

I sat up, rubbing the back of my head. "Go ahead, tell me how wrong I am, that everything I've learned so far is for naught because of... something." My bitterness was leaking out again. I didn't try to restrain it.

Amber sighed, crouching next to me. She'd tied her auburn hair back in a ponytail and was wearing a light set of buckskin leggings and a loose top. "If you think I'm going to take any lip from you, you're wrong. So what if you're a captive here? At least you're alive. The Boss and Crane will come up with some way to set you free."

I grumbled a little but nodded.

"Now stand up and I'll let you in on a secret."

You like secrets, Auwei said, trying to cheer me up.

I did like secrets.

I stood. "Go on then. What am I doing wrong?"

"You're trying to fight like a man."

Well, I had been trained by men, so that made sense.

"If you were as big and strong as Tusk, then maybe that would work for you, but you're not. You're strong and fast, yes, but in a straight fight against Ant you'd never beat him." That was probably also true. I didn't like hearing it, but I couldn't argue the point.

"Come on in!" Amber shouted, and a moment later Silence entered, dressed in practice leathers.

Having filled out a lot from the young man I'd first met, he was still lean, but there was a healthy roundness to his growing muscles. He was definitely all man now.

"You want me to fight Silence?" I asked a bit shocked. He still hadn't graduated to the advanced classes with Jack.

Silence smiled. "Don't worry, I can take it." The grin grew a little. "*If* you can hit me." He'd been more confident lately, but this was downright cocky.

"I saw how poorly little Silence here was doing with Ant and asked to train him myself," Amber said, putting a hand on his shoulder.

He didn't even flinch when she touched him these days. He also wasn't "little" anymore, taller than her by a couple inches, a match for my height.

"With his height and build, I thought it would be better if he learned a more womanly style of fighting. He's excelled at it." She beamed at him and he blushed a little then. Some of the old Silence still remained it seemed. "And we've been working on integrating his avatar abilities into his fighting as well. I think you'll find he's more than a match for you now, with your current style of fighting."

Really?

I was curious.

I picked up my practice sword and set myself.

Silence drew forth a single wooden practice dagger. He

settled into an easy stance and nodded. "Whenever you're ready," he said.

I attacked. I'd thought to disarm him of his smaller weapon, then tap his shoulder to take out his primary arm. I didn't get that far.

I felt his blade run across the sleeve of my practice leathers. I'd blinked and missed his movement. And he wasn't done. The wrist of my sword arm was wrenched and suddenly weak. I dropped the blade as Silence, now somehow behind me, lifted his dagger to my throat.

"Hello Legs," he whispered in my ear.

At any other time, held by him like this, with his hot breath upon my ear, I probably would have felt a thrill, but I was too shocked to feel anything but confusion.

He released me and I stumbled forward.

"How'd you move so fast?" I gasped.

"Turns out, mice are quite fast," Amber said with a hint of a laugh. "Our little Silence has some rather amazing speed. I don't know if he can outrun Jack. We haven't tried yet, but I'm willing to bet it would be close."

Yeah, I had to agree. He'd simply vanished from in front of me.

"And what did you do to my wrist?" I said rubbing it. It ached a little, slightly numb, but feeling was quickly returning.

"That... is my style," Amber purred, a cat-like grin on her face. "Or more precisely, Midnight's style of fighting. She taught me when I was new. I taught Princess and Sparrow, then Silence. And now I'm going to teach you."

I nodded. I suddenly very much wanted to learn this style. If it had just been Amber's style I might not have been quite as impressed, but Midnight... she held a special place of awe in my heart for all her mysteriousness.

"I'm ready," I said, regaining myself. "Where do we start?"

"With no weapons," Amber said. "Toss that sword away. The first thing you need to learn is that your body is a weapon. More than that, if you know how to move in the right ways, you can make your opponent's weapon work for you."

I'd seen someone doing that... It took me a moment to recall Foggy capering around the pirate ship. More often than not, the pirates would hurt themselves or each other rather than him. "Is that what Foggy does?"

Amber laughed. "He knows some of this style, yes, though... he's just... odd to begin with. Never much liked weapons and is very good at avoiding them. Midnight trained him herself, before she went off on her mission. And even she was just a little baffled by his natural aptitude for... chaos."

That sounded right.

"So, my body is a weapon?" I still didn't fully grasp this.

"Well," Amber said with a grimace. "Not yet."

I spent that morning and all of that afternoon learning this strange fighting style. Amber taught me and Silence helped. I was happy to be spending time with him again.

Over the next week I learned more and even began to integrate my avatar abilities into my fighting. I could walk up walls or jump swiftly at or away from an opponent. My jumping also meant I could do strange kicks and leap attacks, which even Amber and Silence had trouble avoiding. I started to see how all my abilities linked together. I was actually anxious for Ant and Jack to return so I could try some of my new moves on them.

But when they did, they had bad news.

I was summoned up to the dome to meet with Ant, Maverick, Crane, and Amber.

"Tell her," Maverick said sounding grim.

Ant spoke. "We passed through Grovner's Green on our way home and heard tell of a strange woman seen around town. She matches the description of the mistweaver. She's close, Legs. We don't know what she's planning, but with you not going out, she may be getting desperate enough to come in."

Well blasted, bloody bones!

I nodded. "What does that mean?" I asked, surprised how steady my voice was. I didn't feel as calm as I'd sounded.

"Ant or Tusk will be by your side at all times, depending on who's around. Perhaps both if everyone's home. We'll be keeping a vigilant eye out for trouble," Maverick said in his no-questions tone. "I hear you've been doing well training with Amber. I want you to keep that up. You may not always have a weapon around to help you. Learn to use all your abilities. You may need them sooner than you'd like."

The next few weeks blurred together. I trained morning, afternoon, and evening, with every member of the House. Ant was still a wall of muscle. I could hit him now, but did little damage. With Jack, surprisingly, I came to see the laziness in his style. He was so quick that I don't think he'd trained as hard as he could. I began to hit him more often as well. Silence was still fast, but I was just about a match for him. Amber I hit occasionally, but still ended up on my back more often than I'd like. Tusk was a brawler and her punches hurt like the Bloody Pits, but I was faster and learned to avoid them quick enough. Fennec was about a match for me in speed and agility, with a hint of extra strength, but my avatar-based attacks worked on him nearly every time. Foggy... Foggy was infuriating. Amber was right, he was just naturally averse to being hit by anything. And he couldn't really teach me his style; it was so erratic it suited only him. Princess and Sparrow both surprised me. Neither liked to be in a fight, but both could defend themselves exceedingly well. I practiced a lot with Sparrow to learn her "flighty" defensive style. I couldn't mimic all of it, but I learned a few things. I didn't get the chance to fight with Maverick or Crane; they were too busy trying to figure out the larger picture of what was going on.

Most nights I was exhausted and went to bed, bruised but instantly asleep.

So went the winter.

Until... one late winter day, an unnatural fog billowed up around Hedgewild.

This was it: the mistweaver was coming.

I had to hope — had to pray — I was ready.

The entire crew was home and gathered around me. Gloomy day turned to blackest night and the Mists began to seep in through the tiniest cracks in the house and fill all the rooms and corridors.

She was here.

CHAPTER 22

THE NIGHT DREW ON. ALERT AND WARY, WE WAITED IN THE dome room atop the central tower. The fog which seeped into the house billowed up the stairs, but stopped — a wall of billowing grey — at the entrance to the dome.

"Hunh," Maverick said bemused. "Apparently the dome is *actually* warded."

It seemed so, since the fog came no farther into the room.

Everyone surrounded me, ready.

But as the night lengthened, I could see the signs of fatigue start to show, after hours of taut alertness.

"Rest in shifts," Maverick commanded. He sat on the edge of his desk running a whetstone over the edge of his heavy-bladed arming sword, calm and serene, almost meditative.

Crane had a long straight cane she kept on her lap as she too sat calmly.

Ant, Fennec, Foggy, and Princess took the first rest.

The night stretched deeper.

I wore thick wool pants and a wool top that came to midtorso, a heavy cloak over my shoulders. I'd come to accept that using my abilities meant leaving my midriff open. Also, to wall-walk I needed to keep my feet uncovered. I was glad for the thick carpeting, and the fires in the hearths which helped to keep us all warm.

Silence came to me, whispering, "can we talk?"

I nodded and the two of us moved to the far side of the dome, away from the stairs. There was no carpet here and we were far from the fire. My feet were a bit chilled on the cold stones.

When he spoke, I no longer had to strain to hear him, his voice was full and strong these days. He'd grown so much. "I know we haven't seen each other a lot these past few months. I've enjoyed training with you, though."

He sighed and smiled. "I just have so much to learn and the more I learn the more I see how much more I need to learn." He took my hands in his, held softly between us. "But I wanted you to know, Legs, that... I love you. I know what love is now and I know that's how I feel for you."

"And you're not just saying this because one or both of us might die tonight?" I asked. It was partly a dark joke, but partly not. Our previous moment together, before the Noble's Test had been a high-stress time as well.

He sighed. "I'm *saying* it now because of the danger. But I've felt it for some time and just not known how to say it... until now."

I nodded. I understood. The trouble was, I'd felt so disconnected from him recently. He'd obviously been thinking about me, while I'd thought we were drifting apart. That meant I didn't know how I felt in this moment.

He saved me the trouble, leaning in for a soft, quick kiss. Then he whispered, "You don't have to say anything. I know we've been apart a lot lately. I didn't say this to put you on the spot, only to let you know how I feel." He gave a faint smile. "Perhaps, if we both survive the night, then we can talk more, yes?"

That sounded great to me. "Yes, thank you."

We returned to the sitting area with the others. No one made any comment about our little escapade. Still, I was even more agitated after that, not only worried about the mistweaver at our doorstep, but my confused feelings for Silence as well. I sat, hands distractedly spinning out silk from my belly-button, forming it, then tossing it into the fire.

This tension is killing me, I admitted to Auwei.

Waiting can be an effective tactic of the enemy, Auwei quoted one of the texts I'd read on warfare. *Keeping a foe in a suspended state of tension wearies them. The attacker needs only wait for the right moment to strike.*

You're not helping.

Then get some sleep and—

Yeah, I don't think I could sleep.

Then find some way to relax. Or you'll be spent before the fight even starts.

She was right.

"Someone say something," I spoke into the silence. "I need a distraction." I rose and began pacing.

Maverick spoke, gruff but quiet in the stillness, trying not to disturb those who were resting. "Maverick House has only existed for eleven years. Before that, it was Gander House. I was a senior member of Gander House, so were Crane and Midnight." He gave a short breath of a laugh. "Midnight was the most senior of us. I don't know how old she is, but she's... well the rumor is she's half-Fey."

"Fey?" I said surprised. "The Fey are real?"

Yup. I don't know why you'd be surprised. You have a glowing being of energy inhabiting you. What's so surprising about an ancient race of long-lived beings?

Good point.

"Oh yes, they're real. They have secret towns and villages in the forest east of the Shattered Lands. Some say the Shattered Lands were created in a war between the first mistweavers and the Fey. With the North destroyed, the Fey moved closer to human lands, and some are said to come south occasionally. Rarer still, sometimes they fall in love with a human. Given how old I know Midnight must be, yet how young she looks, and also the fact that she meets most known descriptions of the Fey: short, hair like night, eyes that glow, and skin pale as death." He shrugged. "Seems likely to me."

The rhythmic stroking of his whetstone over steel was almost soothing as he continued. "Anyway, she didn't want to lead the House, neither did Crane, so it fell to me." A long inhalation and sigh of a breath. "There were a few other members of House Gander who chose that time to disperse or retire. That's always an option when a House changes. So, it was just us. Then... Fin was the first, then Amber and Ant and so on." He rose and wiped down his blade, testing it. It was amazing how smoothly he wielded the heavy sword, with just one hand; mesmerizing.

"Before Gander, was Twitch, his was a cricket avatar. Before Twitch was Revel, some form of small dog if the stories are true. And before Revel was Mantis. This House has always been a haven for—"

An ear-splitting shriek split the night as a column of mist shot out from the stairwell to form into a woman in front of me. She held a dagger in her hand as she materialized, and it was at my throat a moment later, slashing.

My training saved me, evading without thinking. I tossed

the webbing I'd had in my hands at her face as I flipped backward. As soon as I landed, I leaped again and this time caught myself high up on the dome, hands and feet attached firmly.

Spirits, the glass was cold!

But you're safe!

And the fight below was... intense. The woman had dissolved into mist as soon as I'd fled and was now weaving around the others, half-there half-not, trying to get to me. The others attacked when they could, but their blades and fists passed through the mist-woman. She materialize to strike at one or another, but the hits weren't meant to kill, only disable. And she was lightning fast. She had Fennec and Princess out of the fight quickly.

Ant's next attack passed right through her. She wasn't staying solid long enough to hit. And as mist, she could move with incredible speed to another spot amidst the group.

Tusk took a dagger-wound to her side, though seemed to shrug off the hit, bashing with her heavy mace, which passed through Hazra. The mist sped to Sparrow and solidified.

I screamed.

Sparrow wasn't there a moment later, quickly flitting away as a bird, as the mistweaver slashed through where Sparrow had been.

Silence could match the mistweaver for speed and, whenever she attacked him, he evaded her attacks with ease.

Mist and attack. Mist and attack, the woman was relentless. Then the mist launched up toward me. She materialized in mid-air, dagger slashing and taking my cue from

Sparrow I shrunk to a spider in an instant. The blade passed harmlessly over where my neck had been.

She kicked at the glass to squash me, but I jumped away, leaving a strand of silk behind.

The mist followed.

I was nearly to the floor when she reached me and materialized. But Ant was there and caught her leg. With a vicious spin, he threw her across the room. She was mist before she hit the far wall.

"Go!" he shouted at me.

I turned human and leaped again, back to the dome.

She came at me again, but I'd learned a lot in the weeks since her last attacks and I was able to evade her. Also, it seemed that — perhaps because of the warding on the room — she wasn't able to use her mist to grab at me like she had on the pirate ship. She could turn to mist to move around, but had to attack physically with her dagger.

I jumped once again, landing on the warm stones of the hearth, seeing how the others had gathered near there.

The mistweaver materialized, but didn't attack me, she went for Crane.

Her mistake was assuming Crane was unarmed. She struck at Crane, who blocked with her cane. Then, with a twist and slide, Crane had a slim-bladed sword in her hand, pulled from the innards of the cane itself. She struck with amazing speed and the mistweaver shrieked again as blood blossomed on her leg.

"Stop!" Amber said, attracting the woman's attention... and that was it.

The mistweaver looked into Amber's eyes and the command sank in. Hazra froze and the dagger fell from her limp grip.

"The iron!" Maverick shouted and everyone was shocked

into action once more. The only known way to bind and contain a mistweaver's power was with iron bands, which others quickly fastened around the mistweaver's neck, wrists, ankles, and waist.

Amber released the enchantment on Hazra and the mistweaver fell to her knees with a keening cry. She was trying to shift into mist, but couldn't move beyond the confines of the irons around her.

I crawled down from the hearth, returning to the floor, but stayed away from the others. The cold stone beneath my feet, less of a concern now as my blood was pumping hard, my body hot from battle.

"Is that it?" I asked, wary.

I believe so, Auwei answered.

"Yes, she won't be able to escape now, or use most of her powers," Crane said. "Careful, though, she may still be able to affect herself." To evidence this, Hazra put a hand over the wound on her leg and mists seeped out of the hand to mend the injury.

"You may have caught me, but I'll tell you nothing!" she hissed.

"We'll see about that," Maverick growled, low and lethal. "Take her to the dungeons."

"We have dungeons?" I asked, blinking. In all my wanderings of Hedgewild, I'd not seen such a place.

Everyone looked at me like I had two heads.

"Yes, of course we have dungeons," I answered my own question. This estate was meant to be the center of peace and justice in the south. So, we'd need somewhere to put criminals.

Ant and Tusk hauled the mistweaver to her feet and took her away as the mists outside began to disperse. It was almost dawn, faint light in the east.

Maverick stopped me before I could leave.

"Legs," he said softly. He seemed concerned, jaw tight and tense. "I... that seemed a bit too easy."

Had it?

It had seemed like a bloody nightmare to me. But I trusted Maverick's judgment.

He continued, saying, "Just... watch yourself."

I nodded. "I will."

Silence came to me, throwing himself at me in a strong embrace. His words were a bit muffled from his head buried in my shoulder. "I'm so glad you're alive. I'm so glad *I'm* alive. I *feel* so alive! I love you, Legs!" I held him close, tight. I didn't know what to say in that moment. The only words I could find were,

"Thank you," I whispered them softly and he seemed to accept that.

As I left, I asked Auwei: *Maverick said that seemed easy. Did that seem easy to you? She almost had me at the start there. I was terrified and... the others were hurt and... and yet, we had* caught a mistweaver, some of the nastiest known villains in history. Perhaps...

I too am worried, Auwei said, hesitantly. *This isn't over, I can feel it. But... we did capture her, so that's something. Just remember, there may still be others out there who want you dead.*

Right, yeah, thanks. Some Nobles of my own nation were trying to kill me.

Not the most encouraging thought.

CHAPTER 23

IT WAS LATER THAT SAME DAY, THAT RAVEN, A MEMBER OF THE Royal House, arrived with a message and a mission.

The woman, wearing a black cloak, with blue-black hair to match her name, was taken to see Maverick directly. After she left, flying away as her avatar, several of us were called up to the dome.

"I don't like this," Maverick started. He shook his head and crumpled a piece of parchment. "This is all wrong, but... we have a mission, and I can't think of any way to avoid a direct order from the queen."

"The queen?" I said, at the same time Amber and Ant did.

Maverick nodded. "Yeah. They couldn't even trust it to a courier or a pigeon." He kept shaking his head. "This feels wrong," he repeated, but then sighed. "Sit and listen."

We did. In the room, aside from myself, were Silence, Ant, Amber, Foggy, and Sparrow.

Maverick paced. I'd never seen him this agitated. He'd been a rock last night waiting for the mistweaver, but now...

Finally, he stopped and looked at each of us. "This

mission is dangerous, far more dangerous than stopping pirates or anything else we've ever done... other than fight a mistweaver. I know why they've given it to me, but I don't like it at all." A sigh. "You're being sent to infiltrate the royal palace of Vauphan, and acquire intelligence on their war effort." He breathed out a heavy breath.

We all sat, stunned.

"War?" Sparrow said, confused. We all were. As far as I knew — as far as we all knew — Elista had a good relationship with its eastern neighbor. We didn't even share that much of a border. There was a bit of hilly forest in the north, not that far from Miraline actually, where the two nations met. Other than that, the nations were separated by Dyrens Bay.

"That was my thought as well," Maverick said. "This is the first I'd heard of it, but Raven was insistent that Vauphan has been threatening the border recently. So far, the attacks have been minor and mostly kept quiet by the queen. But she needs to know what they're up to, hence this mission. She feels they will attack in earnest soon, and needs to know when and how they plan to come at us. Their navy is far stronger than ours and if they cross the bay in force..." He sighed and ran his hand through that thick hair of his. "Like I said, this feels all wrong." He sat and put his head in his hands for a moment.

We all waited for him to continue.

"I'll summon Fin," Maverick said. "You six are the best at stealth, your avatars good at getting into small places. This is a spy mission, keep quiet and keep low. Get in, get the info, and get out." He swallowed hard. "And don't get caught." His jaw twitched. "Because if you are, we'll disavow that you went with our consent. We'll say you're rebels and leave you to their justice." He ground his teeth for a long moment. "I don't like it, but that's how it has to be." He turned away. "It's why they picked us. We have the best crew to do it and..." I could hear the distaste in his voice. "My crew is the most expendable, the least favored. We're perfect."

I could tell he was upset, even if only because the room was getting unbearably warm. Maverick's skin was a bright red, near to glowing with heat. His clothes were smoking. He got himself under control a moment later and the color faded. The room suddenly felt far too cold.

"I won't force any of you to go. I'll take volunteers only."

I had to speak up. "Should I be going?" I asked. I'd been locked down for weeks now.

Maverick gave a harsh laugh. "If anything, you're safer in Vauphan than you are in Elista."

I nodded; that was... confusingly true.

"And we have the mistweaver in custody," he said with a shrug. "We'll be questioning her while you're gone, trying to find out what we can, but I think you're... mostly safe now. And you've been cooped up for a while, so if you want to volunteer...?" He shrugged.

"I'm in," I said. I was terrified, but I was also desperate to get out. This mission, as much as it was dangerous, sounded like it was made for me. With my ability to be a spider and hear through walls and doors, I could easily overhear the right conversation.

"I'm in," Silence said, with far more confidence than I would have expected. Then he winked at me. "Someone has to keep an eye on you."

Ant and Amber spoke over each other. "I'm in."

Foggy laughed. "You're all crazy, I'm out, thanks." Coming from Foggy, that was an indictment indeed.

That left Sparrow. She looked terrified, but then looked

at me and seemed to surprise herself when she said: "I'll go."

I had to smile. It would be good to have her along as a scout.

"Then it's set. We'll head to the coast first thing tomorrow and summon Fin. Get some rest. We were all up late last night."

We dispersed.

Silence followed me until we were outside of my room since his was just a little farther down the hall.

He put a hand on my shoulder, giving a reassuring squeeze, then wordless, moved on to his room.

"Silence," I said, voice hushed and uncertain. He turned back to me. "Would you... like to come in?" I asked, not really knowing what I was asking.

The faint smile on his lips grew and he nodded.

We entered my room and I closed the door, but there we stopped, standing in the entry hall for a moment.

"Legs?" Silence asked, probably curious why we were just standing here.

Why *were* we here? What had I wanted? Why had I invited him in? My feelings around him were still so confused.

Would you like some help? Auwei asked?

Spirits yes, please!

You may be confused, but you didn't want to be alone right now, did you?

No, you're right.

I guess the question is... how do you 'not want to be alone'? Do you want to talk to him? Just be held by him? Or, do you want more?

I wanted to be held, so I started there. "Hold me," I whispered, and he did, stepping in to enfold me in his arms. I put my arms around him too. I was glad he was my height now; I could rest my head on his shoulder without it being awkward.

"You're scared," he said.

"Spirits yes, aren't you?" I whispered. I couldn't recall, so I asked him, "have you been on a mission yet?"

He shook his head, I felt the movement. "No. My training is mostly done, but up till now, I'd always had too much to learn to go out. This will be my first. And yes, Legs, I'm scared."

I probably shouldn't have been. The mistweaver had been captured. This would just be a quick jaunt into Vauphan, a little light spying, nothing too dangerous.

A little light spying? Auwei laughed at that. *You have an interesting way of looking at things.*

"At least a mistweaver won't be trying to kill me on this mission," I said to Auwei and Silence.

He held me closer and I felt Auwei's soothing warmth. So far, every significant fight I'd had as a noble... had been with a mistweaver. That could shake a girl up.

And in that moment, I knew exactly what I wanted from Silence. "Make me forget about that," I asked, voice quiet. "I want to forget about everything for a while. Can you do that?"

"Yes, Legs," he said, then shifted to kiss my cheek.

I lifted my head and my lips found his. After that I let myself go, sinking into my senses, trying not to think.

Strong arms held me. Soft lips kissed me for some time before shifting to press all over my body. Our clothes were shed and we moved to the bed. Silence worked with deft fingers and soft lips between my legs until a powerful orgasm swept through me.

Then I rested in his arms as he simply caressed me,

every touch seared into my sensitive skin. And when I wished for more, he kissed my breasts, bringing my nipples to hard peaks and teasing my clit with his fingers once again. Finally, I begged him to take me. He was hot and sure and thrusting deep as he drove me to the heights of a second release, then joined with me. And when I demanded more, he gave it, freely, finding new ways to thrill me and make the world wash away.

Silence stayed with me that afternoon and night. We lay in each other's arms, except for the times he rose to get us food.

Late that evening, a strange thought occurred to me as I drifted between waking and sleep.

"Have you been with Amber?" I asked, drowsy and content, but... curious.

He gave a light laugh. "No. She asked once if I wanted an... extended education. I declined. She didn't pursue it after that. She still teases me relentlessly, but that's it." Then, with a note of curiosity in his voice, he asked: "What about you, with Jack or Ant or..."

"No," I said before he named every other man in the estate. "Jack offered a *steamy* bath once, but I said no and he left it at that. Ant... he's different. He's a gorgeous man, but he's never approached me... in that way."

"Jack came to me once," Silence admitted. "Asked if I wanted to try something different." He paused for long enough that I opened my sleep-heavy eyes and looked at him.

"And?" I asked.

Silence whispered, "I think, if I didn't have you, I might have... tried... *something different*." He wore an odd grin.

I blinked, as the image of Silence and Jack, two slender and beautiful men pressed together, came into my mind.

Suddenly I was getting quite hot. Curious about this, I said, "Oh?" And hoped he'd elaborate.

"When I lived on the streets, I got to know others who were... down on their luck. I met two men, a couple, who loved each other dearly. For most of my life, they were the only example of love I knew. Because of them, I've always been... curious."

That was interesting indeed. Spurred by some strange thought, I asked, "And if I wanted to invite someone to be with the two of us, a man or a woman, what would you say?" That feeling I'd had, that one person just wasn't enough, bubbled up within me.

His brows rose. "I... don't know. I'd have to think about that."

That wasn't a flat no. *Very* interesting. Somehow that thought helped me find the peace I needed to sleep warm and comforted in his arms that night.

The next morning, light flooded through my windows, waking us early. Silence dressed and hurried back to his room to get ready for the mission.

When I left my room, I saw Amber waiting, leaning against the wall in the hall. "He's always wanted you," she said with a half-grin. "Don't break his heart, Legs." Then she left.

I gaped, then let out a nervous laugh, not fully understanding that woman. I had so many questions. Not the least of which was... how had she known?

Not long later, after a quick breakfast, those of us going to Vauphan crammed into a carriage and headed for the coast. Maverick went with us.

A strange device awaited us on the beach: a large metal disk hanging from a frame, which could be moved down the rocky shore until mostly submerged in water. Maverick moved the frame until a little less than half of the disk was in the water. Then he took a heavy, cloth-headed mallet and struck the metal disk three times. We waited a few minutes, then he struck it again, three times.

A few moments later, Fin appeared on the beach with us.

"You called?"

Maverick explained the mission.

"I know the perfect beach for us, scouted it many times," Fin said, and we all — except Maverick, who would return to the House — took Fin's hands.

A moment later we were on a different beach far away.

Our mission had begun.

CHAPTER 24

I KNEW FROM MY STUDIES, THAT THE CAPITAL OF VAUPHAN was on the coast. I assumed Fin had brought us close, but all I could see was the expanse of beach before us, stretching away to the north and south. Inland, beyond the beach, were stark cliffs. To the south, there was a rise in the cliffs and a rocky prominence of land jutting out into the sea. The beach beneath that part of the cliff was a lot narrower and much rockier.

"The Vauphan capital is on the bay, just around that prominence there," Fin said pointing south. "The Palace is atop these cliffs. You'll see it above you once you're on the other side of that peninsula. From here, you can see some lookout posts atop the cliff." He pointed again. And now that he'd indicated them, I could see the small structures at the top of the cliff south of us.

"If there are lookout posts, should we be hiding?" Ant asked.

"Why? Mostly they're looking out to sea for pirates or ships that might be a threat. We're already on their shores. If they see us, they'd have no reason to think us anything other than Vauphan residents." Fin had a point.

After a moment with no more questions, he went on: "You'll want to get to the top of the cliffs, which, given this group, should be easy. From there, infiltrate the palace and find what you need. I won't be able to go with you, for... obvious reasons, but I'll be here, on the beach, when you're ready to leave."

It took me a moment to figure out those "obvious reasons." Fin was a large man, and his avatar was a whale. There would be no way for him to get up that cliff, but the rest of us, as he'd said, would find it much easier. Sparrow could ferry Ant and me, Amber could fly, and Silence...?

"How will you get up?" I asked him.

He smiled. "I'll climb. Mice are excellent climbers."

"Have you been practicing?" I asked, curious. There weren't many places to climb around Hedgewild, except for some much smaller cliffs of our own by the sea.

"He's been clambering all over the outside of Hedgewild," Amber said. "If he can climb that fitted stone covered in ivy, then he can climb a cliff well enough."

I nodded.

"Do we think it's better to go up the cliff here, and across to the palace?" Ant asked the group. "Or go up right under the palace. It would probably be easier to just get inside if we went in that way."

"I think you've answered your own question," Amber said, voice silken. She was practically purring, a sultry grin on her face. I guessed she and Ant had been together last night. Better happy Amber than catty Amber.

She wore a daring red dress, trimmed in gold and cut to show off her assets. We'd been told to dress up, but still be able to move around easily. The hope was to look like we fit in as courtiers inside the palace. Sparrow sported a lovely dark blue dress. Ant wore a dark green jerkin over a billowing white shirt. Which on him, made him look huge and imposing. His pants were a dark brown, and his boots black, and high, to below the knee. Silence had on a dark blue shirt and black pants. He'd acquired a new pair of boots, which matched Ant's. I was in my green Noble's Test dress. Amber had said I'd be more distracting in one of her gowns — she had a good selection which left the midriff uncovered — but I'd declined. I wasn't ready for that yet.

We walked down the beach to the base of the prominence.

"I'll wait here," Fin said. "Stay safe. If you get separated, return here."

We nodded and began to pick our way over the rocks at the base of the jutting cliffs. It took us a little time to move safely around the peninsula.

Once we had, we could see the city of Vauphan, from which our neighboring country took its name. It sprawled along the wide curve of a round cove further inland, where the land was more level with the sea. There were ships in the harbor, a fleet of large war ships and numerous small fishing boats, but all of that was far removed from where we were. The waters near us were scattered with jagged rocks jutting up from the surface, not safe to sail.

The only thing close to us was the palace and surrounding castle compound, rising from the cliffs above us. We could see it clearly now that we were on the south side of the prominence. Tall towers rose into the sky and stark white walls clung to the top of the cliffs, imposing while still being bright and cheery.

It was mid-morning by then. The sun bright on the brisk late-winter's day.

"Sparrow you're with me," Amber said. "We'll take a look around and see where we want to bring the rest of you." She turned to Silence. "You might as well start climbing. That's going to take a while."

He nodded, moved to the edge of the cliff, then surprisingly veered into his mouse form.

"I would have thought he'd stay as a human, the climb wouldn't seem as far," I said to no one in particular. Amber and Sparrow had already shifted and were flying away, so Ant was the only one with me.

"From what I hear," he said. "He climbs exceptionally well as himself, but far better as a mouse. So, it might be farther, but he'll move quicker and be safer."

That made sense.

Ant sat on a rock, looking out to sea. "Having a mistweaver after you can't have been easy. How are you faring?"

I sat next to him. "I'm still a bit... tense. Somehow, I can't believe it's over, even though we have her in the dungeon. Something..." My hairs all stood on end, my spider's senses perking up as I spoke. "Something doesn't feel right about all of this."

He nodded. "Yeah, I know what you mean. Capturing a mistweaver... should that even be possible?"

I didn't know and didn't answer.

Ant changed the subject. "I'm glad you've been doing well training with Amber."

I laughed, recalling how I'd managed to flip him onto his back the last time we'd sparred. "If I can get you on your back, I must be doing something right. I never thought I'd be able to best you after that first day of training."

He laughed, though the sound had an odd quality to it. He seemed about to say something, then didn't. Instead, he sighed and after a moment laughed again. "I hear you had Silence on his back last night?"

I instantly flushed a deep shade of things-I-don't-want-to-talk-about red, or so I assumed given the heat upon my cheeks.

"Amber told me," he said softly. "She has a way of knowing who's with who at Hedgewild. Some sixth sex sense." He laughed. "There's a tongue-twister."

I still didn't know what to say or why he'd brought it up.

"I just... you two are both young and I know things happen. I want to make sure it's not going to get in the way of the mission or affect you... adversely."

The words were out of my mouth before I could stop them: "Does sex with Amber affect you adversely?"

He didn't react other than to nod. "I suppose that's fair to ask." He looked back out to sea. My question hadn't thrown him at all.

He shrugged. "Some days it does." I hadn't been expecting this level of casual candor from him. "We don't... expect much from each other beyond our beds. She's alluring and sexy, and she thinks I am as well, but we're not really... together. It's mostly just a physical thing. That makes it easy to keep distant and not think about her when she's out on missions." He sighed. "But there are times when I worry about her." He shrugged. "To be fair, I worry about everyone when they're on a mission. Though I guess I have an extra helping of worry for her on occasion."

"It's the same for me and Silence," I said, though I didn't know if I meant it.

Pits! I didn't even know how I felt about the two of us yet!

Being with Silence yesterday had been... amazing, then relaxing and comfortable. I knew I wanted more of that, but my question to Silence about whether he'd be good with others joining us still hung over me.

If he said no... I wasn't sure what I'd do.

I had no words to express how I felt other than confused. I wanted Silence, but also wanted *more*. Worrying for Silence was distracting enough without trying to figure out the details of our relationship. Not knowing exactly what to say, I just echoed Ant's words back to him. "I have an extra helping of worry for him right now, that's all."

Ant nodded. "Good."

But that brought up a point I'd been wanting a bit of clarity on. "What's the official policy on House members being together? Are there... boundaries I should know about?"

Ant nodded, still looking out to sea. "Yeah, we've always been a bit quiet on that," he said. "Officially, there's nothing against Nobles finding a spouse within their House. But each House has their own set of unwritten rules. Sometimes those rules are about who is right for who or when is right for a marriage. We at Maverick House don't regulate people like that, but at the same time, I think we have an unwritten rule that you can fool around a bit, but marriage is... different. Not that Maverick is against marriage. He just wants people to make sure they're right for each other and truly ready for it." Ant sighed. "You didn't hear this from me, but I think that's because he once asked Midnight to marry him and she turned him down."

What?

I didn't say anything, but my mouth hung open as I blinked loudly at Ant for a long moment, wanting more information.

He glanced at me and laughed at my expression.

"Yeah. I heard it from Crane. It was a while ago, when he

was young and she was... well younger I guess, but who knows how old." He shook his head. "Midnight is truly fascinating. You'll see when you meet her. She looks like you or Amber, a youthful woman, but... there's something in her eyes that's... heavy. She's got the eyes of an old woman who's seen far too much." He digressed. "But yeah, the Boss was captivated by her and wanted to make it official. She... didn't. So now there's this undertone around relationships at the House. You can have some fun, as long as no one gets upset or hurt, but if you want more, you make sure you're fully ready. Boss won't allow it otherwise."

"Oh."

I'd just learned far more than I'd expected to, sitting on this rocky beach.

We sat in silence for a while after that.

Sparrow returned and let us know where Amber would be waiting. Then we all veered into our avatars and Sparrow carried Ant and I up, one in each small foot.

I watched the sea fall away as the craggy cliff sped by, higher and higher. I tried not to let the extreme height affect me. Though I found myself spinning out and knitting together a sort of sail with my silk. It was something I'd learned and been working on as an ability, which I couldn't yet do in human form, and had done a couple of times successfully in spider form. If I fell, the sail should flare out and catch me, slowing my descent.

As it turned out, we landed well enough inside an empty room, flying in through an open window. Amber was inside waiting for us. "Good, now that you're here, I'm going to go check on Silence and make sure he knows where to meet us. He may be a while." She veered into her butterfly form, and flitted away. This mission wasn't about time. We'd be able to fit in for a while before someone noticed we shouldn't be here. It was mostly about knowing where to be listening to hear what we needed to hear. That was far more uncertain and meant we might end up being here for a day or two. The hope was that if there was a war in the works — and it was well known — people would be talking about it openly in the palace, where they were safe.

But that remained to be seen.

It took a while before Amber returned and Silence joined us. It was mid-afternoon by then. Sparrow had flitted down to the kitchens and stolen us some bread and cheese.

Once we were all together, we went over the plan. Ant and I would search one wing of the palace, Amber and Silence another, while Sparrow kept to her bird form, flying around to hear what she could. We'd meet back in this empty room at midnight.

Then we were off.

My heart raced as Ant and I passed our first random person, but we exchanged pleasantries and he went his way... that was it. The man hadn't suspected anything.

That helped to alleviate some of my tension.

This just might work.

CHAPTER 25

EVERYTHING WENT WELL... UNTIL DINNER.

A functionary found us in the halls and asked if we'd be attending the dinner that evening in the Royal Hall. I hesitated, but Ant accepted the invitation easily.

"Yes, of course."

And when the functionary asked our names, Ant answered, "we are Lord and Lady Halvarion, in from Walthrick," he said with such confidence, even I believed him.

The functionary nodded and left.

Ant turned to me and shrugged. "Dinner could be a great place to get some information."

"Or get caught," I whispered, making sure no one was around.

He shrugged. "One or the other, I guess we'll see. You know where to meet up if we're separated. That room at midnight, or the beach where Fin left us. If things go badly change into your avatar form and find a crack to slip into. They don't have Lumani here, they won't be able to follow you. But I'm sure it won't come to that. You'll do well at dinner."

"As your wife?" I asked playfully?

"You could do worse."

"I could do better."

"How dare you talk to your husband that way!" He'd said it playfully, but given our discussion earlier on the beach, I was feeling just a little odd about playing the part of his wife.

And at dinner, things didn't improve.

I felt it as soon as I walked into the long hall, a humming tension in the room. Everyone here was on edge. Ant and I got a few curious, sidelong glances, but once again, Ant used that same name, Lord and Lady Halvarion, from Walthrick, and people seemed to accept it.

I pulled him aside. "Who are these people? Do I have a name? Why is everyone so accepting?"

He grinned. "Your name is Lady Ahlana Halvarion. I did some research before we left. The Halvarions are from the north of Vauphan, and fairly reclusive. People down here at the capital are unlikely to know them. We're also fairly insignificant, with a small holding. So, we're a curiosity at best. Oh, and my name is Viktor."

"Viktor, Ahlana, got it."

But then, once word got around who we were, people began coming up to us with a very similar question: "How are things in the north?" Or "Are you worried for your lands?" We answered with generalities and hedging vagueness, which people seemed to accept, but still. I began to wonder... what was happening in the north of Vauphan?

Then the dinner began.

We all sat, and the king and queen entered from the far end of the hall, a proud couple in their forties, but even from a distance I could see the lines of worry and weariness on their faces.

The first two courses were served, which was great, as I was famished, lunch having been a bit sparse. There was a break before the third course, during which the king stood. Everyone looked to the monarch.

The king sighed heavily. When he spoke, his voice was rich and full, filling the hall, yet his tone held a note of heavy fatigue and concern. "We have received word from the Fey of the Ne'erwald Forest. They have agreed to help us in our cause. They can see the threat from Elista as well. They'll be sending several patrols of Haryagars to the front, along with some Kuznmeisters." The king sighed heavily, shaking his head. "I do not wish for what is to come. I did not start this war, but—"

He didn't get to finish as a building murmur turned to startled screams and cries of alarm.

"They're here!" someone shouted. "The Elistans are attacking! Protect the king!"

I tensed, ready for a fight... but no one was looking at me or Ant. They were looking at the unnatural, billowing mist, which was seeping into the hall.

Oh no! Auwei breathed.

Ant and I said it at the same time. "Mistweaver."

"There must have been another besides the one hunting you," Ant whispered urgently. "These people have no chance against one."

He was right. "Neither do we," I pointed out.

Ant nodded. "Things are going to get chaotic in a second. Use that to veer and find some crack in the wall. Get out of here. I'll meet you on the outside. We can't help these people." His voice was hard, it was clear he didn't like what he was saying, but it was the truth.

Guards rushed to the king, while courtiers tried to flee, but all the doors were sealed. We were trapped in here as the fog filled the room, as thick as could be.

"I'd hoped you'd be here," a voice whispered in my ear. A voice I knew *very* well.

I spun and saw Hazra right there beside me.

"How...?"

She laughed. "I'll kill the royals first, then I'll come for you." And she faded into the mists from which she'd come. The fog was all around us now, I couldn't see farther than a few inches.

Blackened bloody bones! My heart thundered in fear. I reached for Ant through the haze, wanting the comfort of his solid presence, but he must have already veered and fled, as he wasn't where I thought he should be.

I slid off my chair and turned into a spider. Finding a table leg, I crawled up that and onto the underside of the table. I felt safe here, at least for the moment.

Ant's words came back to me: *find some crack in the wall. Get out of here. I'll meet you on the outside.* But I didn't want to venture out into the chaos of running feet and swirling mists. I huddled where I was, terrified.

Somehow Hazra had escaped the bonds holding her at Hedgewild and gotten here... and she was going to kill...

Her words finally sank in.

...Kill the royals...

What in the Blackest Pits was going on here? My mind wasn't working. I didn't understand any of this.

I think I'm starting to understand at least part of what's going on here, Auwei said. *Though I still have no idea how Hazra got here. That woman terrifies me in a way I've never known.*

Me too. So, what's your theory? I'm all ears.

Technically you're all legs at the moment. Sorry, I'm nervous and I joke when I'm nervous. Anyway, I think Hazra's attack on Hedgewild was a feint, she let herself get caught so we'd feel safe and you could go on this mission. A mission that came that same day!

Spirits and Sprites, she was right!

The plan was to get you here so Hazra could kill you and the Vauphani royals all at once. I still don't know why we're killing our neighbors, though from what the king was saying it sure sounded like they were preparing for a war. Still, if anything, this will only provoke them more!

Which meant... *If we're discovered here, we'll be blamed for the assassination. We were set up. Someone back home WANTS this war. So... even if I get away from Hazra, I need to make sure I don't get caught... that none of us are caught!*

Agreed.

Horrible screams and the gurgling of the dying began to fill the hall. Spirits! I needed to get out of here. But my eight tiny legs were frozen in fear. I didn't know which way to go, where I might find some crack I could slip through. I'd already lost Ant and...

Something moved beside me and I shifted, skittering away a little.

It was an ant.

Oh, thank the Mists!

We couldn't communicate in these forms, one of us would have to transform back to speak. Ant did so, now crouched under the table.

"I'm going after her," he said, voice hard.

No! Get out of here, keep to your original plan. You can't defeat her alone! I couldn't say it, couldn't stop him. I was too terrified to shift back and speak. He rolled out from under the table and was gone into the mists.

Ant! No!

I was alone again. Alone in a foreign country, where everyone was trying to kill me.

I found a crack in the wood of the table and squished myself into it. Trembling, I waited for this horridness to be over, hoping Ant would succeed, but certain he wouldn't. As a spider, I couldn't cry, but internally I wept with terror and grief.

CHAPTER 26

"Legs?" The voice was low, a whisper, but near... and it wasn't Ant or Hazra, but...

Silence!

"We heard a commotion and came to check it out, I slipped under the door and could smell you in here, are you in spider form?" I saw him crawling along under the table, looking around. "You're close, but I can't see you."

Oh, Silence, go. Get out of here!

He can't hear you. You'll need to change back.

I know that!

He was right beneath me, sniffing around, which looked odd in his human form. "Legs?"

I dropped from my hiding spot onto his shoulder.

He started and looked, then smiled. "I'm so glad you're safe." He spun a tight circle and began crawling back the way he'd come. "This is the way out; I can smell Amber and..." He stopped moving and whispering, frozen in place. It took me a moment to sense what he had, all the little hairs on my spider-body were on end and not twitching at all.

There was no sound.

The fighting and dying that had been happening around me had stopped, and Silence had sensed the lull as well.

A moment later he veered into his mouse form and I fell off his now-much-smaller shoulder. I was too big to ride on him. We cowered, frozen, next to each other.

That's when it occurred to me. If I couldn't hear anything that meant one of two things: either Ant had killed the mistweaver... or she'd killed him. And given a thick fog still clung to the room, I feared the worst.

"Come out little spider," came the sing-song call.

My bones froze, icy claws of fear sinking into my soul.

Silence's red eyes looked at me. Even in mouse form I could see his fear.

And it was seeing that fear — matching my own — that shifted something within me.

Oh... I felt that. Auwei said.

My fear hadn't fled, it remained, but something deep within me had surged up to subsume it. Icy claws of terror still lingered in my flesh, but my soul and spirit were free, and I knew what I had to do.

I shifted back to human form and whispered to Silence. "Get out of here. Tell Maverick the Vauphani are bringing Fey from the north and planning for war. After this assassination of their royals, they'll be attacking us for sure. Also, someone back home set us up to die here, perhaps to blame all this on us! Now go!"

The tiny grey and white mouse skittered away, running swiftly across the stone floor.

I slid out from under the table, body trembling with... something. I didn't know what I was feeling. I was still terrified, but some unstoppable part of me had decided to run toward the danger, not away.

It's called bravery, Legs. Auwei said, proud but terrified.

Don't worry, I'll give you all the benefit of my nine lifetimes, all the things I've learned about combat. But I trust you too. You've trained relentlessly. You know what you need to do.

I huffed a heavy breath and felt my skin tingle, muscles flexing as a thrill ran through me.

"I'm here, Hazra. Come and get me."

A laugh. "Oh, aren't we brash!"

I targeted that voice and threw a ball of webbing.

Another laugh. "Missed me."

I threw another, and another. Following the laughter as it danced around the room. I couldn't see a thing through the blasted fog, but if I could just hit her, hopefully that might distract her long enough for me to get to her.

"You'll never hit me," she chided, sounding distant.

I nearly leaped out of my skin when she spoke next, a whisper right next to my ear: "I am everywhere in this mist."

The combat training I'd been drilling for the last few weeks kicked in and without thinking I spun. My elbow connected with her ribs, even as a blade sliced across my side. It had probably been intended to sink into my back, but with how I'd turned, it caught me a glancing blow instead, across my ribs.

Laughter danced away as I grunted, putting a hand to the wound. It wasn't as bad as it could have been, but it was still bleeding freely. I spun some webbing to place over it, clotting the wound, but it still burned with searing pain.

This wasn't going to work. I couldn't keep still. If she could move freely in the mists, then I should already be dead. Unless she was playing with me. If she hadn't spoken the last time and just stabbed me, I wouldn't have known until I'd felt the pain, and not been able to react as quickly.

I didn't know why she hadn't just killed me, but the woman was insane, so perhaps she didn't know either.

I kicked off my slippers and hoped I remembered how high the ceiling was in this hall. I jumped. If I leaped too hard, I'd crash against the stone above, but too lightly and I'd fall back down. Again, my practice paid off, and I was able to find the ceiling with my hands and stick, then brought my feet up and switched to walking upside down, keeping on the move, planting and placing silk-strands around the room. Perhaps, I could catch her in a web. Unless she actually *was* the fog, then I'd be damned to the Blackest Pits.

What saved me next was pure luck. I'd returned to the floor to place another strand when something slick under my foot — probably blood, but I didn't want to think about it — caused me to slip as she attacked. She'd been trying to slit my throat, but I fell and the blade instead cut my chin, then traced a line up my cheek, between my right eye and right ear, and up into my hair. I instantly veered into my avatar and skittered away, before returning to my natural form to leap back up to a wall. With each new strand of webbing I placed — quivering with the faint vibrations in the air — I was getting more and more of a sense for the room and her movements.

The failure of her last attack must have frustrated her. Her laughter turned to a growl. "You'll not catch me in a web, little spider. I'm done playing!"

The fog solidified around me, crushing me to the floor, then turned sharp, like the points of a thousand nails piercing into me.

I screamed, even as I veered into my spider form to get away from the constricting, piercing pain.

But that last attack had nearly done me in. Even in spider form I felt the wounds all over my body, the slow leak of blood. I'd be dead soon if I didn't find a way to turn the tides.

My hairs pricked up and warned me at the last moment as she materialized above me. I leaped away to avoid her stepping on me.

My hairs...

My spider sense! I hadn't been using it to the fullest. I'd been trusting to my web and my regular hearing to know where she was.

Yes, of course! Why didn't I think of that, Auwei said. *I guess terror got the better of both of us. You concentrate on finding her, I'll do the rest.*

I surged back to my normal form, eyes closed, concentrating on my spider's sense. I gathered as much webbing as I could in my hands and waited, still.

"I feel your life ebbing, spider. You've stopped running. Are you ready to die?"

I felt the voice around me. Each sentence from a different point in the room. She truly was everywhere, but I waited. I hoped my stillness meant she wouldn't use the solid fog on me. I gambled my life on her wanting to finish me on her own with that dagger of hers.

My hairs bristled. I felt the flow of fog as it swirled around me, felt her move within it, and I waited. I wouldn't hold out much longer. I was covered in my own blood, from the myriad of tiny punctures all over my body. I'd be too weak to stand in a moment, then dead not long after. She'd not even need to come for me. That meant I needed to get her attention.

"End this," I whispered, hoping my voice was filled with despair.

"As you wish," she hissed.

I felt — through my spider's sense — her materialize

right in front of me and thrust with her dagger. I sensed her triumphant inhalation of breath...

And that's where I stuffed my handful of webbing, clamping it over her mouth. Auwei did her part, reacting far faster than I would have. She leaped back as the mist-weaver's dagger pierced my chest over my heart. It sank an inch into my left breast before I managed to get away.

I heard the mumbled struggling as Hazra tried to breathe, the raking of her own nails over her face to remove the webbing. I surged back in while she was distracted. My spider's sense knew exactly where she was. I grabbed her arm, the one with the dagger, and forced it into her chest. Then I bashed the hilt with my palm to sink it in deep.

She must have freed part of her mouth as I heard a gasping scream. Then the fog whipped around me. I was tossed into a wall, hitting hard, sinking to the floor as the mists swirled in an agitated frenzy.

Her muffled cries lasted a moment longer as the mists whipped and thrashed and then... they were all sucked back to one spot, to her, as she fell to the floor, dead.

I laughed, a weak sound, surprised I'd actually won. But the laughter quickly faded as I saw the carnage in the hall. The freely flowing blood from dozens of bodies, the dead king and queen, the sliced-up courtiers. It was a testament to how weak I was, that I didn't even have the strength to be sick at the horrid sight.

Then I looked down at myself and saw my torn dress, bits of it falling away exposing far too much skin. But my modesty was a secondary concern, next to the wounds on my chest and side and face, not to mention the tiny bloody punctures, all over my body. I spun some silk to patch the larger wounds, but by that point I was getting dizzy, weak.

The many points of light in the room were fading to

darkness. I slumped to the ground, as a large form drew close to me. I couldn't make out who it was as I fell into unconsciousness. My only thought was: if it's a guard, I'm dead.

CHAPTER 27

"You just refuse to die, don't you?"

I blinked awake, and grunted with pain, my body on fire with a thousand cuts.

Ant leaned over me. "I've healed you as much as I can, without blacking out myself. I think you'll live, but Spirits Within, you're a mess, a tough as nails mess."

"Don't mention nails," I groaned. It still felt like someone had stuck me with hundreds of those blasted things all over my body.

He grinned, but it was a faint thing. He looked incredibly drained and weary. Oddly, there wasn't a scratch on him.

"How...? You're..."

"I think she wanted me to take the blame for all this. I was trapped in solid fog, but left unharmed and alive." His weak grin widened. "So, you saved me." He held out a hand to help me stand. It took a couple of tries and when I finally got to my feet, I leaned heavily against the wall.

"I'm not gonna get far," I groaned. Just standing was a chore.

Amber appeared nearby, probably having inched under a door in her butterfly form, then rushed toward us. She took one look at me and her eyes went wide. "Girl, put on some clothes!" She scooped down and plucked up a cloak from one of the dead, it was slick with blood, but neither of us cared as she wrapped it around me.

"Thank you," I said. "Where's Silence?"

"I sent him back to Fin with your message. Hopefully he's long gone by now."

I nodded. *Good.*

"Let's get out of here," Ant said, picking me up like I was nothing. He even shifted me to one arm, as he easily lifted the heavy bar off the door with his other.

Sometimes I forgot how incredibly strong he was. Ants could lift many times their own weight.

Yet as soon as we were out of the great hall, my hairs pricked up as I caught the distant sounds of running feet... lots of them.

"Someone's coming," I said, voice so very weak.

"Yeah," Ant grunted as he an Amber both tilted their head in a very similar way. I'd learned it was an antenna thing, scenting and sensing the movement of the air.

"Too many," Amber added. "Except... from that direction." She pointed down an adjoining hall.

Ant and Amber shared a look, some unspoken communication passing between them. Then the big man sighed, gave a grim smile, and set me down. "I'll hold them off as long as I can."

"What?" A part of my spirit broke at the resigned look on his face. "No! You—"

"Hush, child," Amber whispered as she tucked an arm around me. "No use arguing when he gets like that. He's tough, he'll catch up. Come." I put an arm around her as she helped me limp down the corridor.

When I looked back, I saw Ant duck into the great hall and come out with a short broadsword. The weapon seemed tiny in his hands. How could he defend himself with something so small?

I turned to Amber, ready to tell her that I hadn't just killed a mistweaver to let my friends die like this, but the words died on my lips. There were tears on her cheeks. I'd never seen her shed a single tear before.

She must have caught my shocked look from the corner of her eye. With a slight shift of her head toward me, she gave that same grim smile I'd just seen on Ant's face. "Yes, I worry too. Now let's get going so his sacrifice isn't in vain."

I nodded.

Despite the healing Ant had given me, I could barely walk. He'd closed the larger wounds, but I was still bleeding — if only a little — from the dozens of small cuts all over me. I didn't move fast and Amber was half-carrying me. Finally, she laughed. "It's amazing what we forget when we're on edge." I didn't know what that meant until she said. "As much as I don't like the idea of a spider on me, could you shift? You'd be a lot lighter."

I laughed too, nodded, then veered into a spider, climbing up her arm as she rolled her shoulders.

"Much better," she said with a sigh. After that, she moved with greater haste through the corridors of the palace.

There were people everywhere: guards running this way and that, terrified courtiers huddled in groups. Nobody seemed to know what was going on, which was good, since that meant few had a moment to spare for a woman in a red dress hurrying through the halls.

It wasn't until she stopped suddenly, looking around, that two guards approached from down a short hallway to her left.

"Bones," she hissed. "I think I'm lost."

"Excuse me miss, you can't be in this part of the palace," one of the guards said. He approached with his halberd lowered just a little, not threatening yet, but ready.

"Yup, bloody bones, somehow I've ended up in the royal wing!" She hissed to herself, and probably for my benefit. She turned to the guards with a smile on her face. "Hello, boys." I saw her look intently into one set of eyes then the other, then she waved her hand saying, "Forget me." And she walked right between the two of them as they stood there, a bit stunned.

I turned around on Amber's shoulder as she casually walked down the short hall, so I could watch what happened to the two guards.

"I thought..." one of them said. "Did you just...? I...?"

The other one sniffed. "I don't know what you're talking about. We should get back to our post."

"Ah... yeah... right."

I thought, when they turned, they'd see us for sure, since we hadn't yet passed beyond the doors at the end of the hall, but their gazes seemed to look right through us.

Amber opened one of the large double doors and entered, and the guards seemed to see nothing. They returned to their places to either side of the door, facing out, as it closed behind us.

I hopped from her shoulder, shifted back to human, and slumped into a large cushioned chair. "What are we doing here?" I hissed a whisper. "We're in the royal chambers!"

She smiled and shrugged. "The king and queen are

dead, it's not like we're going to be interrupted. Perhaps I can find more plans on their war effort. We're really going to need them now. Stay here, I'm going to snoop for a moment. Besides, the Royal wing is on the north side of the palace and opens up onto the top of that point of land. We can escape out there when we're done."

"But Ant... he won't know where to find us if we're not—"

"Don't!" she hissed, spinning back to me, lips tight and trembling, tears threatening. She lowered her voice when she continued. "Don't say his name, please." She drew in a deep breath and stilled her tears. "He'll know where to go if we're not in the room. He'll find Fin, and so shall we." She gave a valiant attempt at a smile. "We'll all meet there." And with that she spun and walked into one of the many rooms off this large main living area.

I didn't realize I'd fallen asleep until a voice woke me. "By the gods!" the voice was male, not Amber. At first, I thought it might be Silence, then I opened my eyes and was gazing up into two of the most beautiful blue eyes I'd ever seen. Well-kept raven black hair framed a face that still held a hint of youth upon firm, manly features.

I didn't know how much time had passed, but the room was dark, lit only by a lantern on a nearby table.

"Who are you?" the man asked me.

"Le—"

Not your real name he's not an ally! Auwei shouted at me.

"Lei—ana?" I hadn't meant to make it sound like a question but I wasn't fully awake yet and also... still only a few steps off from death.

"Leiana?" he said, then smiled. "What happened to you? How did you get here? What's that on your face? Do you know what happened in the palace? I haven't heard—" And a look of fearful uncertainty crossed his face.

My mind finally spun back to life and I realized who this young man must be. He looked like the recently dead king. This was the crown prince!

And I... I was a foreign agent, lying in his suite, dress torn to shreds with a borrowed, blood-soaked cloak not quite covering me. Then, there was the patch of spider-silk over the side of my face. Yeah, I must look a Pits-spawned sight indeed.

I blinked, feigning ignorance. "I... I don't know. I was attacked, then saved by some men who pulled me in here."

His face grew more concerned. It was clear he had no idea what was happening outside these rooms. He looked at the double doors. "I should call for the guards."

"No! Please. Just... stay with me for a moment?" If the guards came in, they'd not know how I got in here, given Amber's influence. And that would only create more questions, since I would have had to pass them to get here.

I started to rise, though that wasn't easy, and reached up to him. I put a hand behind his neck to help me up and to pull him down. I needed to distract him and the only thing that came to mind was a kiss.

He gave in, allowing me to draw him closer and even putting an arm around me to help me up.

Our lips touched. His were soft and full, and I pressed against their warmth for a long moment... until his entire body went oddly stiff, too tense.

I tried to pull back, but his arm behind me wouldn't budge. I could see confusion and panic in his eyes.

Something was wrong.

In order to slip out of his hold, I had to press my body against his in a most intimate manner as I shimmied to the side. Once I was out of his embrace it was clear he was frozen, completely immobilized, only a few muscles twitching.

Oh... Auwei breathed. *I... I think we've just found a new power.* Her tone was somewhere between bemused, confused, and horrified. *Some spider bites can cause paralysis, and your kiss is... sort of like a bite?*

I could tell she was trying not to laugh, though it was an I'm-sorry-for-you, pitying laugh.

"Bloody bones!" I hissed the curse. "Really?" *But then why didn't I do that to Silence when we...?*

I don't know, but my guess is that you felt something far different when kissing Silence and this was more of a survival instinct, so... yeah.

That made sense. The trouble was, I didn't know how toxic my poisoned kiss might be. I didn't want to accidentally kill the crown-prince. Oh wait... he was the king now. "Bloody bones!"

Yeah.

"Who's he?" I spun at the sound of Amber's voice. She had a satchel stuffed with something, probably important papers.

"The crown prince. I... I think I poisoned him... by accident. I kissed him... to distract him... and I think I have poison now...?"

"Isn't that just the topper?" She grimaced. "And it's new, so you have no idea how bad it is." She nodded to herself. "Blasted bloody bones!" She was thinking, her eyes shifting, probably trying to figure out what to do. I was still too weary to come up with any ideas.

"Pits... bring him with us," she hissed.

"What?" I didn't think I'd heard that right.

"We don't want to kill him, and if we leave him, we don't

know what will happen. Yet, if we bring him back with us, we can hopefully find an antidote and give it to him. Either way, we need to go now."

"I can't carry him," I grumbled.

"I can, he's not that big. But I can't carry both of you, so can you shift?" She slung the satchel over her shoulder and came to us. I veered into my spider and hopped onto the prince who Amber picked up roughly and slung over her shoulder.

Amber left the lantern and moved slowly through darkened rooms out onto a balcony.

Stars twinkled in the night's sky above us as Amber navigated a set of stairs down to a long roughly triangular, walled garden, which I recognized as the top of the jutting peninsula. It was deserted as we made our way to the edge. There was an awkward moment, during which I had to shift back and help Amber get the body over a low wall at the top of the cliffs.

It was only when we stood upon the bit of land between the wall and the sheer drop, that we realized our problem. I could walk down the side if I needed to and Amber could fly... but the prince...

"Use your silk, it's strong enough to support a person, yes?" Amber said.

I nodded. We laid the prince on the ground, his eyes the only thing moving, and I wound him up in my silk, ensuring I had a good hold.

"Sorry about all this," I said to him. "We didn't mean for any of this to happen. We'll fix you up and send you right back. I promise."

"I'm not sure if your diplomacy means much after poisoning him," Amber said.

True. "Ready," I said. "Can you fly out there and make sure he doesn't hit anything too rough on the way down?"

She nodded.

I wove the many strands of my silk, which held the prince, into a heavy rope and looped that around one of the stone merlons atop the low wall. Then, I fed out my silk to lower the prince. I used my own weight as a counterbalance, my bare feet on the wall to ease the tension on me. Injured and exhausted, it took everything I had to hold the prince steady and lower him slowly. It seemed to take forever. My arms began to burn with fatigue, then turned soft, like jelly. Still, I held on. I didn't know how I was managing to do any of this in my condition, but didn't question it. Then....

A flapping of wings, and Sparrow appeared beside me. "Need help?"

"Oh, Spirits, yes, take this line!"

She did, bracing herself as I had, and taking over bearing the weight as I let out more and more silk. Then finally we felt the line go slack. We waited, resting, until Amber appeared next to us.

"Sparrow, good, carry Legs down." To me she said. "I made sure he went down smoothly and landed softly." Good. "Now let's get out of here!" She was back in her butterfly form in an instant.

I became a spider. Sparrow picked me up and we were all soon at the base of the cliff.

Sparrow helped Amber carry the prince off the rougher rocks, to a more level stretch of beach where it would be easier for one person to carry him.

And we didn't have to carry him far, as Fin moved out from the shadows of a shallow cave into the moonlight.

"Ready to go?" he asked. "Where are the others?"

"Ant will be coming," Amber said, stalwart. "And Silence should be here already, was he not?"

Fin shook his head. "You three are the first."

"Well Pits," Amber said vehemently.

My gaze shot up to the top of the dark cliffs above us. Silence hadn't arrived? Where was he?

My heart lurched. Now we had two people missing.

CHAPTER 28

Fin returned us to the great hall of Hedgewild. None of us liked leaving the others behind, but someone had to report what we'd found and the crown prince still needed help.

Fin vanished after returning us, going back to the beach to wait for Ant and Silence. I sat heavily on a bench and laid my head down on a table. The prince was laid out on another table and Amber and Sparrow then ran in different directions to get the others. Amber had mentioned that Crane knew something of medicines and there was an herbalist in Grovner's Green, but otherwise... the person who knew the most about poisons... was Midnight and she wasn't going to be of any help here. Ant might also be able to heal the prince, but...

I couldn't think about that.

I was in pain and overwrought with worry for Ant and Silence, yet still my exhaustion won out and I must have dozed, for I woke, sitting bolt upright when I heard a groan.

I looked over at the prince. Something seemed different.

His body is relaxed, not rigid anymore. I think maybe your poison is wearing off.

Auwei was right. He seemed less rigid and when he shifted, groaning again, I knew he was coming out of the effects of my toxin.

I should probably apologize.

You may want to wait for the others.

No, he's fine now, we don't need Crane. I rose, aching and weary, and made the short trip to the next table, slumping down on the bench.

"Prince?"

He rolled his head over to look at me. His face grew hard. "You're not going to kiss me again, are you?" His words were a little slurred, but understandable.

"No… and sorry about that. I didn't know that was going to happen."

He raised a single brow. I don't think he believed me. He rolled his head back to look straight up.

"I'm in Elista?"

"Yes."

"You've captured me?"

"No, well, I don't know. We brought you here to help you. I didn't know what my poison did to you and in case it was worse than just paralysis, we wanted to help you."

He nodded. "Why were you in the palace?" he asked.

Ah… what should I say?

Got me, I wouldn't have talked to him at all. Maverick should be handling this.

Oh… right, yes, that makes sense.

"I can't say right now." But… there was something he deserved to know.

Legs, wait, it may not be best to tell him about his parents.

He needs to know. And he needs to know it wasn't us.

But it was us, it was Elista. The mistweaver was from Elista!

Oh... right. But still...

It's up to you, my child.

Up to me.

I put my head down on my arms, which rested on the table, and groaned.

"Are you well?" he asked.

I looked up. "No. I was hurt, a lot... trying to save your parents." That wasn't entirely true. I'd just been trying to survive. But I'd killed the woman who killed his parents, that was worth something, wasn't it? Still, I glossed over the story a little. "A madwoman from... from Elista, she went to kill your parents, and probably you too. We... ah, we went to stop her. And we *did* stop her, but... not until it was too late. She was too strong. She... your parents..." I didn't know how to say it. I looked up to see him trembling.

"They're dead?"

"Yes."

A single tear left his eye, sliding down the side of his face into his ear. "But you fought one of your own, tried to stop her?"

Well, not exactly. "Yes."

"That's why you're all cut up?"

"Yes."

"Don't say anything else!" Maverick commanded as he strode into the room with Sparrow, Jack, Fennec, and Foggy. "Either of you. I'd prefer not to start an international incident over a casual conversation." He strode over to stand over me and the prince. His gaze lingered on me for some time. "You well?" he asked.

"Somehow, yes," I answered. Though I must have looked

a mess in my shredded dress and bloody cloak, with spider-silk webbing over my face.

His mouth twitched a half-grin for the barest of moments. "Tough little one, aren't you?"

"I guess so."

He turned to the prince. "You're not dead?"

"It would seem I am not. I was just... immobilized for a while." He rolled his head to the side and looked at me with a clear we-know-whose-fault-that-was look.

Maverick drew in a long breath. "We can't return you right away. We're sorry for the trouble. Once our transporter returns, we'll—"

"I've been thinking about that." The prince's tone was weary and tentative.

"Oh?"

"It seems someone from Elista is trying to kill me." The prince lifted his head enough to look around at all of us. "But clearly none of you are. In fact, from what I've heard you've been trying to help? You may have saved me? I'm less certain about that, but I know this. If you wanted me dead, I'd be dead."

Maverick nodded, saying nothing.

"So... why *don't* you want me dead?" The prince sounded truly confused and curious.

"We have no quarrel with Vauphan." Maverick's tone was even.

"Then why have you been annexing our northern territories for the past three years?"

What?

I looked up at Maverick in shock, but it was clear he knew nothing of this. He seemed to be struggling with this news as well. Finally, he nodded to himself. "Your Highness, I knew nothing of such attacks. It would seem someone in

Elista is doing this without the consent of the Council of Nobles."

The prince nodded. "We'd wondered about that. It did seem... odd." He sighed. "But with the attack on my parents, it certainly seems like Elista wishes to declare war on Vauphan." He grunted as he sat up. It seemed my poison wore off in stages and he was still weak, having trouble controlling his movements. "Or at least, *someone* in Elista wants war, if not the entire country. He looked directly at me, then Maverick. "What are your intentions, Lord Maverick?" So... the prince knew his Elistan Nobles. Interesting.

"I wish only peace between our countries, Your Highness."

The prince nodded. "Then I'm going to stay here," the prince said firmly. I'll need to coordinate a few things with whomever remains at the palace, and find some way to communicate with them, but... if there is indeed someone in your country trying to kill me, this is the last place they'd expect to find me, isn't it?"

Maverick nodded. "We'll have a room made up for you, Your Highness."

"And while I'm here, please don't call me 'your highness.' You can call me by my name: Alvere."

Maverick nodded. "Yes, Alvere." He turned to Sparrow behind him. "Have a room made up, please?"

She nodded and hurried off.

Maverick turned to Fennec and Jack, saying: "Please make sure nothing happens to the pri— to Alvere. I need to speak with Legs."

I stood.

"Legs? That's your name? You said it was Leiana," the prince said with a grin. His eyes dipped down to my — now mostly exposed — legs and he smiled. "Never mind, Legs suits you."

I'm fairly certain I blushed at that, then pulled the blood-soaked cloak about me and followed Maverick out of the room. He led me to a room stocked with supplies and grabbed several rolls of linen bandages. Then we went to my room, which I hadn't been expecting. Stopping at the door he nodded his head inside, holding out the bandages. "There should be some water in there, clean yourself up and get dressed. I'll wait."

I took the bandages and went in.

It took me a while to do as instructed. I removed the ruins of my dress and looked at myself in the long looking glass. I was a supreme mess.

Gently peeling away the web-bandages I found the larger cuts mostly healed: Ant's work. There would be scars, but I didn't mind that. I was alive, that's what counted. Then I carefully used a rag to wash and clean the other small wounds... which were everywhere, it looked like a thousand nails had stabbed me. Some were healed, the rest weren't deep. Still, the cuts stung when cleaned, and some re-opened and bled a bit more. Then I began bandaging myself with the linen Maverick had provided. I did one leg, then the other, a bunch around my midsection and chest, then — the hardest parts — my arms. There weren't any cuts on my face that weren't already closed or healed by Ant.

I was incredibly stiff, so I found a loose dress, put it on, and went back out to Maverick.

He looked at me, shook his head, then motioned for us to go back in.

He sat heavily in a chair and I did the same, a bit more gingerly.

"Amber tells me you killed the mistweaver?" he said, right to the point.

"Yes, was anyone hurt here when she escaped?"

He tilted his head with a curious expression. "That's what you have to say? You kill a mistweaver and you're worried about *us*?" He grinned. "I knew I liked you. I made a good call selecting you. Yeah, we're good here. She didn't escape. Turns out we didn't have her at all, but a duplicate of some sort, a façade over someone else. That someone else is still in the dungeons, but they stopped looking like the mistweaver earlier today."

That was interesting.

"Back to you. How are you doing?" he asked.

Exhausted.

Achy and itchy.

Bleeding.

A soul-weary and emotional mess.

"Well enough. I'll survive these cuts and... well... mostly I'm worried for Ant and Silence."

He chuckled. "Yup, you're a keeper. Clearly in pain but worried about others." He shook his head slowly. "The mistweaver may be gone, but someone out there still wants you dead. We'll need to be careful." A sour grimace twisted his lips. "Though I think that goes without saying now that we have the prince visiting."

He rolled his eyes. "You have a way of bringing trouble to my House, little one. First a mistweaver, now the prince of an enemy nation. What next, the Emperor of Thraan and his host of dragons?" He grimaced. "Don't answer that. I don't want to know."

He leaned forward, running both hands through his thick, messy hair while blowing out a long breath. "I honestly don't know what's going on. Someone... someone high up in the Noble Houses is killing Lumani and invading Vauphan and somehow managing to keep it all quiet. There has to be some plan behind all of this, but damned if I know what it is."

He looked up at me then with a wry grin. "But I know one thing. Whatever their plans are, you're going to ruin them." He laughed. "All I have to do — and you're not making it easy — is keep you alive long enough to do so."

He rose and made his way out, stopping at the door, half turning back. "I'll let you know if Ant or Silence returns. For now, get some rest." He paused then shrugged. "Your standing orders are... stay alive at all costs. Got that?"

"Yes, Lord Maverick."

"Good."

He left, and I stumbled over to my bed, but as exhausted as I was, I couldn't sleep. This bed only reminded me of Silence.

So, bone-weary, I rose and made my way back to the great hall. Most of the members of the House were there. The Prince and Maverick were not, but Amber, Jack, Fennec, Foggy, and Sparrow were sitting around talking in hushed voices. And shortly after I arrived, Crane came in from the kitchens with warm soup and hot tea.

She gave me a cup and a smile.

Then we all waited.

It was hours later, near dawn, when Fin appeared. With him was Ant, who was a bloody mess and barely able to stand. The big man sat on a bench — a bit too heavily — and broke it, collapsing to the floor. Amber ran to him, tending to him. She peeled away his shirt, gasping and shaking her head as Sparrow came with bandages to help.

"Silence?" I asked.

Fin shook his head slowly. "Not yet. And..." He looked around. "Where's the Boss?"

"He's with the prince," Crane said, coming over to take a look at Ant. "Why?"

"Before Ant arrived, I saw two or three dozen ships setting sail across the bay. They'll be on our shores tomorrow." Fin's face was hard. "I think we're at war."

Don't miss the next book in the series!

SHAPE AND SHADOWS
The Mists of Elista Trilogy, Book Two

I kidnapped a prince and started a war... what else could go wrong?

I may have... accidentally... kidnapped the prince of Vauphan. Not to mention, the Vauphani people think I killed their king and queen, but I swear I didn't do it. I was trying to save them... sort-of... not that anyone there will listen to me. That ship has sailed, along with a small fleet on its way to Elista in retribution.

And my small noble house is all that can stop them.

As for me... well, the man I love is missing and I think I may be falling for that prince I kidnapped (which was totally an accident, I swear). Things only get more confusing after I sleep with my best friend. It turns out, she wanted to be more than friends.

Now I just have to figure out whether I want Silence, my friend, a prince, or all of them (is that possible? I hope so) while surviving more attempts on my life, saving my sister, and stopping a war that I swear I didn't start.

OTHER BOOKS BY CLARA WILS

THE GRECIAN GODDESS TRILOGY

written with Tessa Cole

Kiss of the Goddess, book 1

Power of the Goddess, book 2

Bonds of the Goddess, book 3

THE MISTS OF ELISTA

Bonds and Blood, book 1

Shape and Shadows, book 2

Form and Fury, book 3

SHADOWS OVER ELISTA

Double Discovery, book 1

Double Danger, book 2

Double Disaster, book 3

Double Doom, book 4

Double Destiny, book 5

SECRETS GODS KEEP

written with Tessa Cole

Craving Demons, book 1

Chaos Demons, book 2

Claiming Demons, book 3

www.ingramcontent.com/pod-product-compliance
Lightning Source LLC
Chambersburg PA
CBHW030142200626
46812CB00015B/809